Holidays & Homicide

A Paranormal Witch Cozy Witch Mystery

Book Store Cozy Mystery Series
Book 5

Lucinda Race

MC Two Press

Editor Kimberly Dawn
Cover design by Mariah Sinclair

Manufactured in the United States of America
First Edition November 2023

Print Edition ISBN 978-1-954520-70-7
E-book ISBN 978-1-954520-69-1

Author's Note

Hi and welcome to my world of cozy mystery.

I hope you love my characters as much as I do. So, turn the page and happy sleuthing . If you'd like to stay in touch, please join my Newsletter. I release it twice per month with tidbits, recipes and an occasional special gift just for my readers so sign up here:
https:// lucindarace.com/newsletter/
and there's a free cozy mystery when you join!

Happy reading…

**Special note to my readers: My books are drawn entirely from my brain. AI was not used in the creation or editing of this book.

1. Robin's Cafe
2. Bygone Antiques
3. The Pembroke Cliffs
4. Cozy Nook Bookstore
5. Twisted Scissors Hair Salon
6. Betty's Market
7. Old Town Libary
8. Miss Judy's Dance Studio
9. The Sweet Spot Baker
10. Bee Bee's Boutique
11. Tuckers Hardware Store
12. The Copper Kettle
13. Police Station
14. Town Hall

Chapter 1
Lily

QUICK NOTE: If you enjoy Scares & Dares, be sure to check out my offer for a FREE bonus at the end. With that, happy reading!

* * *

Tightly closing the door to my bookstore, I hurried down the brick sidewalk in the direction of the police station. But my destination, The Sweet Spot

Bakery. Across the street I could see the holiday decorating committee was busy putting the final touches on the decorations around the ice skating rink. The annual holiday Winter Glow and Glide skating party was from seven to nine tonight. This was the first time Gage and I would be going as a couple. I looked at the glove on my left hand, saw a distinctive bump on my ring finger and sighed. We had been engaged for six weeks and it had been the best time in my life. The snow was blowing and creating drifts in the square, and I didn't want to get pulled into a conversation with the volunteers. The store had been busy with holiday shoppers but I needed a quick pick-me-up, and it was easier to zip down Doenut Drive and past the police station to reach my friend William's bakery. And if my handsome fiancé's car, who was also a detective on the force, was in the parking lot, I'd take a quick detour and see if he wanted to join me for coffee. As I rounded the corner I noticed his parking spot was empty.

Pulling the hood of my wool jacket up and

tugging on the laces, I braced myself against the freezing cold. The snow was picture-perfect for the holiday season and about time. I thought about how the first storm historically arrived right after Thanksgiving, but not this year. It was mid-December and this was the first measurable snowfall. A sharp toot of the horn caused me to look up, and I waved to Archie Dane, our mailman. His mail truck glided to a stop beside me.

"Hi, Lily, where are you headed?"

Archie's wide smile always elicited a grin from me as he gave me a friendly wink. "Kinda cold out to be taking a walk." Bright-red wool gloves were a sharp contrast to his blue uniform jacket which was neatly pressed. His short brown hair was partially covered by a blue knit hat with the USPS logo on the front. He looked as if he stepped from a recruiting poster for the post office. Well, except for the red gloves. They were downright practical for this weather.

"It's refreshing and hopefully it will bring

people out to skate tonight. I'm not sure if you've heard, but Robin's Cafe is donating hot cider and cocoa, and The Copper Kettle and The Sweet Spot are hosting a cookie corner."

"I'm looking forward to it. I've sharpened my skates and am ready to take a few turns around the ice." He looked at the police station behind us. "Will you and Gage be coming?"

My heart sighed. It was the first year that we'd be skating as an engaged couple after all the years we'd been just best friends. It had taken me almost dying at the hands of some crazy lady, and a few close calls for us to open our eyes and state our true feelings. "We're looking forward to it. I just hope I don't spend more time on my backside than my feet."

He said, "I've been walking around my house to practice wearing them again." A wistful look splashed across his face. "If only I hadn't lost at the state championship, who knows how far I could have gone in the world." Tugging on the front of his jacket, he said, "But then I wouldn't be here making sure the mail arrives on time to my friends and neighbors."

I wanted to offer him sympathy that all works out for the best, but knew that no real words would comfort him. Never having experienced that type of setback, I decided to ease away from the topic. "Are you bringing someone with you tonight?"

The smile was back. "Noelle Webber. I met her a few weeks ago. She's a driver at We DOT Shipping. We met delivering a package to the same place, and then I bumped into her again at the Magical Moonshine Pub in Robin's Pointe—that's where she lives. I think it was fate."

I was genuinely pleased Archie had met a nice girl. At least I was assuming she was since he deserved someone special. "I'm looking forward to meeting her tonight."

Gripping the steering wheel, he said, "I'd better get going. Mail delivery needs to get done so I can get to Robin's Pointe and back in plenty of time to take Noelle for dinner before the Glow and Glide starts. It's her first time skating, and I'm hoping she enjoys it."

"I'm sure she will with you by her side." If I hadn't been paying attention, I wouldn't have noticed the corners of his mouth deepen to a brief frown. "Yes. I need to get my coffee and get back to the store. With Christmas two weeks away, I'm in for a hectic day."

Saying goodbye, Archie tapped the horn one more time as he pulled away. I watched as the small white vehicle took a left turn on Route One, leaving town and not heading where I thought his route went. I did feel bad for whatever was troubling him. The next time I got the chance, I'd ask him, just to make sure there wasn't trouble that I could help him fix. I pulled my collar close to my face and hurried down the sidewalk. Winter in New England had finally arrived.

· · ·

I was getting ready to lock up my bookstore for the day when the front door opened. Milo, my familiar, sat up on the front counter where I was working and said, "Well, look who's here; it's Detective Cutie."

My fiancé was tall and well built, with the dreamiest hazel eyes and light brown hair. I could see from where I was standing his vintage cherry-red pickup was parked next to the curb. He crossed the room with a swagger full of confidence but not cocky. "Hello." Gage's deep voice warmed my heart. His voice held the same smile that was on his lips. Leaning in, he kissed me.

"Hello, yourself. I thought you were picking me up at home?"

His finger trailed down my cheek and gently pushed my chin up, tilting my face to him. "I couldn't wait another minute to see you."

My heart sighed as this kind of talk could potentially sway me from going skating, but I knew as a shop owner I needed to be at the event to support the town. "I'm glad you did."

Milo started hacking up a hairball. "People can see you through the window." He jumped down, trotted to his window seat, and then hopped up and settled onto the cushions.

Ignoring him and looking past Gage as the darkness fell, I said, "Did you see the tree in the square?"

He glanced over his shoulder. "You mean the lobster traps stacked to resemble a Christmas tree?" He smiled again. "It's hard to miss with all those twinkle lights and shiny baubles."

Now, I sighed loudly. "I think it's a wonderful idea, and it will save a tree, and it's in plain view of my shop so I can look at it until after the New Year."

Cupping my cheek, he grazed my mouth with his. "I think the view inside is much better. Maybe we should stay in tonight."

Laughing, I gave him a little shove. "Why, Detective Erikson, are you trying to divert my attention away from tonight's event?" I knew that was exactly what he was trying to do. The last time there had been a major town event, someone had been killed, and of course, I started investigating. Solving it had been one of my finer moments, but Gage would never agree since I almost became a ghost.

Straightening, he said, "Can't blame a guy for trying."

I shooed him away from the counter. "Let me finish up, and we can go back to my house and have a quick bite of dinner. I want to get to the rink early. Archie Dane is going to introduce us to his new lady love. He said she's from Robin's Pointe."

He wiggled his eyebrows. "I wonder what she's like. Any idea how they met?" He took a chocolate kiss candy from the jar next to the cash register, unwrapped it before handing it to me, and then he took another for himself.

"They were both delivering a package to the same place, and they clicked instantly from what he said." I popped the candy in my mouth, letting it melt on my tongue. I loved the creamy and sweet treat, and Gage indulged with me.

He twirled a finger around my face. "I hope Archie's girl gets the same expression when he gives her a piece of chocolate." He pecked my lips and a flirtatious gleam filled his eyes. "Are you sure we can't skip skating? It's pretty cold out, and it might snow again."

"Gage, you're incorrigible. Now, make yourself useful and either pick up dinner or sit in that wingback chair and wait for me to finish. The more you distract me, the longer this takes."

Holding up his hands in surrender, he said, "Fine, fine. We'll go skating, but you're buying me a cocoa, maybe two."

I arched my brow and gave him a look that said, *really?*

"Or I'll buy." He laughed. Sitting in the chair, he asked, "How was business today?"

"Brisk, and not a single thing out of the ordinary happened." I finished putting the cash in the money bag and slid it into my tote. "Okay, I'm ready. I'll go out the back and meet you at the house."

"Come on. I'll drive you home. The roads are slick and we can pick up your car later."

That was an offer I wasn't going to refuse. My Mini Cooper was great in the snow because it sat low and wide to the ground, but riding with Gage was more appealing. "Milo, are you coming with us?"

"It's better than getting wet paws tramping through the snow." He landed with a soft thud on the floor and waited patiently next to the front door.

I locked up in the back room and grabbed my coat, hat, and mittens. Now I was ready. Going back into the store, I said, "Let's get this party started."

. . .

After getting cocoa coupons from Gil Akers, Gage and I glided around the outskirts of the rink, holding hands and grinning like teenagers. The turnout was fantastic; it seemed like most of the town was here. I was surprised to see Chet Harvey at the cookie station, helping William pass out sugar cookies. I waved to Aunt Mimi and her husband Nate, my best friend Nikki and her fiancé Steve, and Ellen Pease and her teenage son, Wyatt. I could see my folks looking more like kids than my parents on the opposite side of the ice, grinning from ear to ear.

I poked Gage in the ribs. "Look, there's Archie with his girl, and he's wearing his Santa hat. How festive!" He casually looked in the direction I had indicated. I held up my hand and gave them a wave. "Come on. Let's skate over and meet her."

Taking the direct route, we made a beeline across the ice to where Archie was helping his girlfriend stand. She seemed to be a little wobbly as her ankles bent in before she straightened them again, showing off the skates with bright red laces, and then promptly sat down on the bench.

"Hello." Puffs of frozen air danced between us. Extending my hand, I said, "I'm Lily Michaels, and this is my fiancé, Gage Erikson."

Archie was beaming. "This is Noelle Webber." He dropped his chin and looked at her with wide eyes. "My girlfriend."

He frowned and I glanced in the direction he was now glaring. Chet Harvey and Gil Akers were in his line of sight, and Ellen was slightly behind them. I had to wonder what that was all about, but I turned to chat with Noelle. She had long brown hair and bright blue eyes, and from her sitting position, she seemed to be taller than me.

"Hi." Her voice had a breathy quality, almost as if she was shy. "It's a pleasure to meet you. Archie's been talking about tonight since we met. He said I just had to come. It is the highlight of the holiday season and all." When she looked up, her eyes locked on Archie. "So far it's been fun."

He pulled her to a standing position and her ankles bowed in again. He slipped an arm around her waist and said, "Don't worry. I won't let you fall."

Smitten was the word that came to mind and it seemed to be reciprocated. "It was really nice to meet you, Noelle. Enjoy your evening, and don't forget to get a cup of cocoa. Regan, who owns the café, is running the stand and it always hits the spot."

Archie said, "Thanks," as he pushed off, holding her tightly to wind their way around the rink.

Watching them for a minute, I glanced at Gage. "Noelle seems nice but quiet, but I think that will suit Archie." My attention was drawn to Aunt Mimi, who was waving at us to join them. "Come on. I'll let you buy me a cocoa now, and we can see what my aunt is all excited about."

We glided to a stop next to the cocoa stand

where Mimi and her husband Nate were. "Hey there." I kissed her cheek. "Are you having a good time?"

Aunt Mimi and I looked very much alike, except she was in her mid-seventies with silver gray hair, but at one time it had been chestnut brown like mine. And you'd never guess her age by her youthful grin and spirit and the mischievous glint in her brown eyes. She was a witch. Now that I knew our family was part of the Pembroke Cove witches, I wondered if that was why she always looked exactly the same She never aged, or maybe it was just good genes.

Nate grinned. "The best time." He glanced at the sky. "The stars are out and our Christmas tree is stunning."

"How many of those lobster traps are yours, Nate?"

He beamed with pride. "A good many, and it was fun building it. Not so much fun when we have to deconstruct, but I'm not going to think about that tonight. Right now, it sets the perfect tone for our little seaside community."

Aunt Mimi said, "I'm having your parents over for brunch next Sunday. Please tell me you'll come. I've already invited Nikki and Steve too and of course Gage's parents. I just love this time of year and we have so much to be thankful for."

I wasn't sure if she was talking about the engagement or the fact that I escaped an untimely death four times in the last six months. Gage asked, "What can we bring?"

"Just yourselves." She gave him a kiss on the cheek. "Now, you two should take another spin around the ice before the night gets too cold."

"Yes, Aunt Mimi." I gave her another kiss and did the same to Nate before taking the insulated cup of cocoa from Regan and slipping my arm through Gage's. Over the next couple of hours, we made our way around the ice. We chatted with my parents, Gage's mom and Dad, and Nikki and Steve. They all confirmed they were going to Mimi's on Sunday. As we made one final turn on the ice, I tipped my head back and looked up at the stars. "It is a perfect night."

Gage glanced at the thinning crowd. "It seemed everyone had a good time."

I took his hand. "It's the holidays. What could go wrong?"

Chapter 2
Lily

"Sweetheart, I'm sorry. We should have gotten my car when we left the rink." Gage was navigating the dark side street with ease as he pulled up behind my blue Mini Coop. "All I was thinking about was my frozen toes."

He clasped my hand on the seat between us. "I would have come over in the morning and picked you up."

I gathered up my bag and gloves and kissed him lightly before pushing open the door. "Just give me a minute to get the car started."

"I was going to follow you home."

"No need." I kissed my fingertips and fluttered them in his direction. "See you in the morning."

"Put your gloves on." He shook his head. "Drive carefully and call me when you get home."

I gave him a thumbs-up and dashed to my car. I didn't want a repeat of frozen toes again tonight. My car started up with a gentle hum, and I buckled my seat belt, pulling on my gloves before I went any further.

I looked in my rearview mirror and saw Gage was waiting for me to pull out ahead of him. I did, and when we reached Doenut Drive, he went right and I turned left. I drove around the perimeter of the town square and noticed a light on near the cocoa stand. That was odd. Everything should be shut down, lights off, and the stands locked up for the night. I slowed the car and pulled to the curb. Sliding my window down, I listened. The night was eerily quiet except for the clock in the old church that was chiming eleven. Turning off the car and pocketing the keys, I hurried across the fresh blanket of snow, my footsteps silent.

"Hello," I called out as my heart rate quickened. Drawing closer to the cocoa stand, all of my senses were on high alert. I called out again, "Is anyone there?" I exhaled in an attempt to remind myself that not every time I walked into a scene where things seemed amiss, something bad was about to happen. Peeking around the corner, there was no one in sight. Relief washed over me like an ocean wave. Someone forgot to turn off the light. I walked behind the counter and stumbled, righting myself with a steady hand on the counter. As my hand hovered over the temporary switch, I gaze slid across the ice. The relief I had felt dissipated like air from a fast-deflating balloon. Lying in the middle of the ice was a person.

Rushing around the counter, sliding over the ice, I called out, "Hey, are you okay?" I sank to my knees and eased to a spot a foot away. "Archie Dane." A frozen red river flowed away from his body. He was definitely not okay. I wanted to reach out and check his pulse, but the lack of color in his face had me keeping my distance. Hastily, I withdrew my cell and hit the speed dial number for Gage.

He didn't even have a chance to say hello when I blurted out, "Come quick. To the ice rink. Archie Dane is dead."

The siren wail broke the stillness, and I crouched on the ice next to Archie. I took a bunch of pictures on my phone since this would be my only chance to get them. My teeth began to chatter, and I was chilled to the bone, but I wouldn't leave him.

Dax and Gage skidded over the ice, and he held out his hand, wrapping his arms around me. "Are you alright?"

Nodding, I said, "Yes, but Archie isn't. He's dead. As much as I hate to say this, he was murdered."

Dax was standing next to us. "He could

have just slipped and hit his head."

I looked at him as the sadness washed over me. "Not likely." I pointed to the woman's figure skate near him, the blade coated with blood.

Gage tightened his arms around me, but I couldn't feel the warmth of his body. What were the odds that I would find another dead person in our charming small town?

With my eyes locked on Archie's lifeless body, I asked, "Are Sharon and Mac coming?" They were two of Pembroke Cove's finest and were people I trusted. It didn't hurt that Gage thought highly of them as well.

"Yes. Peabody will pick up Mac on the way here, and it will be up to them to gather evidence and take pictures before we move Archie." He began to steer me away from poor Archie. "Let's get you to a bench and you can tell me what made you stop. I thought you were going straight home?"

Before we left the ice, I took a moment to turn in a slow circle as if taking mental pictures to review later. But nothing seemed out of place except for the solitary light at the cocoa stand. I took one last look at the ice, tipping my head from side to side. Why were his hands bare and where his Santa hat? "Gage, his hat and gloves are missing."

"They're probably in his vehicle," Dax said. "We'll check it out."

He stayed next to the body as Gage and I walked carefully across the ice and sat down on a bench where Archie was helping Noelle with her skates just a few short hours ago. "Why would Archie have taken his date home and then come back?"

He rubbed my gloved hands between his to get the blood flowing again. "Maybe they came in separate cars, or they had a tiff, and he took her home early."

My eyes widened. "What if she's hurt around here and needs help." I tried to get up, and Gage held me in place. He waved Dax over as Mac and Sharon crossed the ice.

"What's up? We're just getting started."

"Lily wants to make sure that Archie's date isn't close by and possibly hurt. Can you have a couple of the uniformed cops take a look around? Just to be safe."

"Yeah, I can do that." Dax glanced at me. "Anything else?"

It was amusing that he deferred to me as this investigation was just getting started. But in my defense, we had become close, like a brother and sister. After the haunted house event and being held at gunpoint our bond was forged. It was also when I discovered he was a powerful witch. "Will you let me know if they find a Santa hat and a pair of red wool gloves?"

His eyebrow shot up. "Our victim's?"

"Yes, he was wearing the hat earlier and the gloves he had on this afternoon. Since they went with the theme, I figured he'd be wearing them too."

"You got it." Dax strode across the frozen surface like he was wearing ice cleats and it was easy to guess he had cast a spell to keep himself upright.

I watched as Sharon and Mac moved around the lifeless form of the mailman. Bright flashes of light popped off at regular intervals as they took pictures, documenting everything from all possible angles. "How long before they move him?" I wanted to hang around as long as possible to see if there was any evidence under his body. And the figure skate that was next to him, what was it about that skate that niggled at me? I grabbed his arm. "Gage, the laces are red and not from blood."

He gave me a quizzical look. "I'm not following you."

"Tonight, Noelle's skates had red laces. Remember when Archie was helping her stand and her ankles kept giving out? I noticed her skates then and rentals would have had white laces. So, for someone who didn't know how to skate, it would have been likely she would have rented them."

"Lily, maybe she bought them because she was going on a date."

It was kind of logical but Gage had never

been inside a woman's head when she was getting ready for a date. "Only someone who knew how would go to the trouble of adding red laces. It's a statement to the world—look at me." I tugged at his hand. "I need to find Noelle Webber and ask her a few questions." I tried to hurry across the ice, but Gage's hand tightened on mine. Turning, I asked, "What?"

He dropped his gaze and took a step closer. "You're not going to investigate this murder. I appreciate your keen eye, but the way this person killed Archie was violent."

I nodded. "And personal. To get up close like that, Archie had to know who it was. She, or he, knew exactly what they were doing."

"Which is why I want you to leave the sleuthing to me, but I know if I have a question that has me stumped, I can ask your advice." He tapped the middle of my forehead. "You have the best mind I know for solving puzzles, but I wish you'd stick to the New York Times Sunday crossword and let me do my job."

I looked over my shoulder to where the

emergency personnel lifted Archie's body onto a gurney. "He was my friend and when we talked today, you should have seen how excited he was to be dating someone he believed was very special. I can't remember a time when he was this happy."

Gage slipped an arm around my shoulders. We both watched as the white blanket covered the gurney was wheeled off the ice. "He was my friend too and I promise we'll find the guilty person and arrest them."

Once the scene was clear, Gage and I crossed the ice to where Dax was talking with Sharon and Mac.

Mac gave me a tight smile. "Hi, Lily. Sorry, you got tangled up in something like this again."

Sharon gave me a somber look. "You certainly do have a knack for stumbling across crime scenes." She shot Gage a frown crossed her face. "Sorry, boss."

"Peabody."

Why everyone called Sharon by her last name still puzzled me and one of these days I'd ask her about it. But tonight, I was bone-tired and cold, and I wanted to go home. "Will someone be able to clean the blood off the ice before morning? It would be upsetting to people in town to see where Archie was attacked."

Dax said, "As much as I like to keep crime scenes intact as long as possible in case of new evidence, this might be the exception. With the holidays and it being smack in the center of town, there isn't any way to preserve it. If Peabody or Mac can meet me here at sunrise, we can do one final sweep, and I can get the ice cleaned before most of the town is aware this happened."

"Really?" I asked Dax. "Do you think this hasn't already hit the phone tree? By morning, everyone will know what happened, maybe even more than what you know." I gave a pointed look from Gage to Peabody and Mac before my gaze rested on Dax. "We're talking small-town gossip at its best. But there are children to consider."

Peabody gave me a wink. "You should think about running for mayor after that little speech."

"Come on, Ms. Mayor, I'll walk you to your car." Gage turned me around in the direction of my Mini Cooper, and Sharon said, "You should follow her home, Gage. Whoever is responsible could know that Lily was the person who found our victim."

I started to say I had my protection spell in place, but before I could blow my cover as a witch to non-magical people, he said, "That's a good idea. I'll be back before you know I'm gone."

Sharon seemed pleased he had taken her suggestion. "Take care, Lily."

When we were out of earshot of Sharon and Mac, I said, "Maybe I should tell them I'm a witch, one of the few in town, and I'm perfectly capable of taking care of myself."

Gage chuckled softly. "Do you remember you've had four close calls, and each time, we've successfully explained how you didn't get hurt and not even hint at magic?" He had a point as we reached my car, and he opened the door. "And it might be easier on some level, but what would that do to my job? I could be kicked from the force, and you—well, who knows what would happen to not just you but all the witches in the community."

I stood on my tiptoes and brushed his lips with mine. I didn't respond to his statement since there weren't any holes in his logic. Instead, I said, "Are you following me home?"

"Yes, I am." He tapped the end of my nose with his cold fingertip. "And before I leave, I was hoping you could magic up a couple of thermoses of hot coffee for my team. We have more work to do tonight if we're going to release the rink in the morning."

I slid behind the wheel and laughed. "You're taking your life in your hands with my coffee, but I'm happy to lend a hand for the cause." I could start the clue board while the coffee was brewing, and yes, I would do it the non-magical way to buy a bit more time pumping Gage for any ideas he might have. I might not be actively involved in the case right now, but when the time came, I was going to be ready.

Before he closed my car door, he leaned in and looked me in the eye. "Drive safely, but don't worry, I'm right behind you."

He closed the door and tapped the roof to signal I should get going. As I pulled away from the curb, I glanced in my rearview mirror, and there was a shadow near a stand of trees, but when I blinked, it was gone. Had it been a person or was it merely the way the trees were leaning? In the morning I'd come back and take a look around. I discovered that the professionals could miss important clues.

I gripped the steering wheel tighter as I saw the ambulance ahead. What a shame. Archie was a good guy, and he didn't deserve to have his life cut short. I knew what I had to do. No matter what Gage was hoping, I was going to grab my proverbial magnifying glass and go in search of clues.

Chapter 3
Gage

When I got back to the rink, I was carrying a tote from Lily's house. She had made two large thermos jugs of hot coffee and even scrounged up a box of store-bought cookies in her pantry. Of course, that was after she pulled out her clue board and set it up. Even when I requested that Lily keep her distance from the case, I knew that was like putting out a blazing fire with a squirt gun. I loved everything about her, and I wanted her safe, but she also needed to be happy and fulfilled. All I needed to do was keep one eye on Lily and the other on the case.

Dax looked up and a grin filled his face as I got closer. He knew not to expect baked goods, but the coffee was hot and fresh, nothing at all like what was waiting for us at the police station. "How's Lily?"

"She's good and you might have guessed she set up her clue board and jotted down notes before I got out the door."

He laughed and took the tote from my hands. Withdrawing the box of peanut butter cookies, he grinned. "Perfect. I could use a sugar zing."

He whistled to get Peabody and Mac's attention and made a drinking motion. They acknowledged they got the message with a wave of a flashlight. They were making a circuit of the outside of the rink which bordered a small row of hedges. I asked, "Did you find anything while I was gone?"

He shook his head. "No. I was hoping we'd stumble across the other skate, but the good news—or bad, depending on which way you're leaning—is, we didn't find Noelle Webber either."

Relieved to hear we didn't have two victims, my thoughts drifted to my suspect list and she was at the top. "I'd like for you to run over to Robin's Pointe in the morning. Lily said she was a delivery driver, but I don't think she knew who Noelle worked for. If Lily does, she didn't mention it. You know the drill. Swing by Noelle's house, and see if you can discover the name of the company. It's the only lead we have at the moment."

Dax had filled a cup with coffee and handed it to me before filling one for himself. "What was our victim like? Mac mentioned he was a mailman."

"I didn't know him well. He was friendly but quiet and seemed good at his job. He always stopped at the station every day at ten on the dot. Lily knew him better so you can ask her, but that's not a great idea either. It will kick her investigation itch into high gear."

He laughed. "And what makes you think it isn't already?"

I knew Dax was right. Even if she hadn't set up her board, there was no way she wasn't fully invested in solving the case. "I couldn't stop her from trying. I only want her to be careful. Even with Nikki as her sidekick, Lily still manages to get into dangerous situations."

Dax said, "It's a good thing she's learned her self-protection spell and it's something that can be strengthened in any situation. She'll just need to be able to focus for it to be effective."

I was curious about how some of this worked, considering our line of work. "When you're in a dicey situation, you can cast a spell?"

His face grew thoughtful as steam curled up from his coffee. "I made it a habit to never let them weaken, but in the heat of the moment, I'm not sure if I could have enhanced them. Those moments are stressful and as a new witch, her discipline and focus aren't honed yet. But if you want, I can work on that with her."

It was an excellent idea, but Lily might hate it. "I'll give it some thought, but if you want, feel free to mention it. Actually, she might be more receptive if you did. But do me a favor, keep me out of it. The last thing I would want is for Lily to think I don't have faith in her abilities."

"Gage, you realize she's only scratched the surface of her power, right?"

Peabody was sliding over the slick surface. She was holding a clear evidence bag in her hand. I nudged Dax so that he wouldn't say anything more about witchcraft. I had no reason to think Peabody was magical, so I did my best not to mention that my mother or Lily, and many others in town were witches. "What did you find?"

She glided to a stop in front of us and handed me the bag. "A note to our victim."

I turned it over and read it before handing it to Dax. "What do you make of this?"

Meet me at ten. Don't be late. No excuse is accepted!!!

"Cryptic but to the point. And I can say it's a good assumption this was delivered to our victim since it has a smear of red on it, probably blood." He handed it back to Peabody. "There wasn't anything else near it?"

"No, it was caught on a branch of a bush. I only saw it after I got on the ground and trailed the flashlight beam on the underbrush."

"Good work." I withdrew my cell and took a couple of pictures so I could review them later and print one for the board at the station. Now, I had to wonder, what was a mild-mannered mailman doing meeting someone here, at the rink, after it was shut down for the night? I thought back to the conversation earlier tonight between me, Lily, Noelle, and Archie. There was nothing that struck me out of the ordinary. There were a nice couple having a good time. I wish I had paid more attention to the way Noelle looked at

Archie. At the time I was more curious about the way he was looking at her. Could Lily have noticed something off with the woman? Her observation skills were excellent, and I'd ask her about it when we had coffee at her bookstore tomorrow.

Peabody said, "I'm going to head over to the other side and join Mac. We'll take one last look before calling it a night. There isn't much around in the way of evidence and Dax mentioned that he was going to make sure the blood magically disappeared before people started coming down to be lookie-loos."

I tried not to react when she said the word magic while turning to look at Dax.

He shrugged. "It's not that big of a deal. I'll scrape it up and toss the mess in a bio bag and dispose of it properly."

Peabody was satisfied with that answer. I knew her off-the-cuff remark was closer to the truth than she knew. "Good. Dax, if you need some help, let me know."

He said, "Yeah, stick around. The two of us working together can get it done much quicker."

"Grab some cookies from the tote and take a thermos of coffee with you. It will help warm up you and your partner."

She tapped two fingers to her knit cap in a military salute. "Thanks Detective, and tell Lily I said thanks too." Slipping and sliding, she got to the tote and then called to Mac that she had fortification.

Despite the seriousness of the situation, it was good to see these very different cops had bonded. Peabody had been with the force for over a year, and Mac was a veteran, but they bounced off each other and it worked. Kind of like me and Dax, but he was from a federal agency, and I had always been a small-town cop.

"Do you miss the old days when you were like them?"

It was always good to answer a question with a question when I didn't have anything to add. "Do you?"

Shaking his head, he said, "Are you kidding? We're not missing much. We have a bit more experience, but they'll be us someday."

I pulled a picture of the note up on my phone. "Why do you suppose people chose to meet here? It's a public space. Anyone could have seen who Archie was meeting."

"You're being very literal. Don't assume whoever 'they' are had this spot as the meeting place. It doesn't say meet me at the rink, or for that matter even meet me at any place specific. All it says is ten and don't be late. If we think this note was one the killer sent to Archie, we need to dig into his background. Was he a person who was habitually late to places? What skeletons are in his closet? Does he have gambling debts? Maybe this has something to do with his job."

I scoffed at that notion. "He was a mailman driving around in his little mail truck six days a week. There was nothing about his job that was hinky."

Dax laughed. "Is hinky a technical police term these days?"

"Funny. But you know what I mean. He goes to the post office, gets envelopes and packages, and drops them off day in and day out to businesses and private homes. No matter the weather, Archie delivers the mail and I even said he was always on time. So that comment in the note about not being late doesn't jibe with the Archie I knew." However, there was one thing about this job—people were never who I thought they were, and Archie might have been hiding a deep, dark secret. One that we'd have to uncover if we wanted to get to the bottom of why he was killed in such a public manner.

"Then maybe he sent the note to someone else and based on the tone, it didn't go over well. They got into an argument and the aggressor lashed out with the skate and that was it."

Dax had a good point about Archie being the sender and not the receiver. "Why use Noelle's skate and where is the other one?"

My cell pinged with an incoming text from Lily. *Check the post office parking lot for his car.*

He drives an older brown Jeep that's got some rust spots on the back fenders.

I shook my head. "How does she do that? Is she clairvoyant?" It was a rhetorical question, but I stole a look at Dax and one shoulder popped up and down. Pushing that thought aside, I focused on Lily. I reassured myself. *We've been friends for twenty years and have spent so much time together, that it's natural she can read my mind.*

"Are we going to search for his Jeep?"

I flashed him a grin. "Of course. Without Lily's message, I was going to have to look up what Archie drove, but now we can zero right in and find it." We walked gingerly over the ice until we got to the exit by the cocoa stand. I slowed my steps. "Why was the light on?" Before we left the area, I needed to look around. I was sure the team had done a thorough job, but I wanted to see with my own eyes. This is what drew Lily to stop so leaving a light on felt deliberate. Whoever did this wanted Archie to be found tonight, but why was the unanswered question. Pausing in front of the cocoa stand, I could picture Regan behind it, hustling cups of cocoa and cider to skaters waiting. The countertop looked to be about three feet long and the shelves behind the stand were tidy with stacks of thermal cups. Three coffee urns that she used for the beverages were turned upside down, waiting for refills. I flipped up the end of the counter top and stepped behind it. There wasn't a lot of space for more than two people. I turned to my left and the ice stretched out in front of me.

"Hey, Dax, can you flip the light switch on the side of the stand?" He did as I asked and the stand went dark. The lights around the town square cast shadows over the rink. In the dim light, I wasn't able to see the spot where Archie was found. This didn't answer any of the questions that were in my head. Maybe finding his Jeep would.

"Nothing clicked?" Dax asked.

"The light had to be on in order for anyone to discover Archie." I walked the two steps to where I had entered and my foot caught on something. The last thing I needed to do was make a mess of Regan's space. I pulled out my cell and turned on the flashlight app. "What the heck?" I knelt down and tried to push a tote bag onto the shelf and realized I was looking at the logo on a navy bag for the United States Postal Service, all four feet by three feet of it. Instead of pushing back, I pulled it out and dropped it on the counter.

Dax turned the light on and handed me a pair of latex gloves as I took off my winter gloves. "I don't have a large enough evidence bag for this one in my pocket." With gloves in place, I cautiously opened the bag expecting to see envelopes, magazines, and postcards. There wasn't anything out of the ordinary in front of me.

"We need to process this and then get it back to the post office."

Dax handed me a large bag that appeared from the inside of his jacket. He bobbed his head in Mac and Peabody's direction. "If anyone's watching, they'll think I'm overprepared." With a flick of his wrist, the bag opened, and I slipped the mailbag inside and secured it. "I'll ask Mac to take this back to the station."

"Good, and we can continue the search for the vehicle." I snapped a picture of the bag, and then Dax crossed to where the officers were packing up. After they talked for a minute, he met me at the exit of the park. One side of the street was empty, but at the end near town hall, at the edge of a circle of light, was a vehicle. Could we be lucking out and already discovering the Jeep?

Dax withdrew a wand from his coat pocket and held it by his side. I glanced at it and he said, "Multipurpose tool."

What that meant I didn't need to ask. As we got closer, I reached for my sidearm but remembered it was locked in a safe at home.

"I've got this." Dax stepped in front of me. He tapped on the driver's window. "Hello. Pembroke Cove Police." He rapped harder the second time and tapped the end of his wand on the door handle and it opened.

Noelle Webber was slumped over the steering wheel.

I asked, "Is she dead?"

Chapter 4
Lily

The next morning, I woke still tired, having slept in snippets. I had continued to turn over the events of last night in my mind. At some point near dawn, I finally drifted off, unable to make sense of why someone would want to hurt Archie. Waking with a start, now I was running late as I hurried to get dressed and scooped Milo from the bed. "Come on, fluff ball. We have work to do and a murderer to find."

Milo arched his body in my arms and groaned. "What's the hurry?" He flipped over and gracefully dropped to the floor and trotted into the kitchen ahead of me. More than likely he'll start demanding I feed him his breakfast first. To keep him happy, I tapped the button on the coffeemaker on my way into the pantry to get him a can of tuna and a box of oatmeal for myself. It was going to be busy and I'd need a good breakfast to power through until Gage brought coffee and maybe even a muffin. After the holiday I was going to buckle down and start exercising again.

"It's the shoppers that we need to be ready for. But I'll have a bit of time to get some research done about Noelle Webber before I open the shop. Also, when we get to town, I'll wander around the rink just in case something was missed during the night and so no one catches me."

"You mean snooping, right?" Resting on his haunches, watching me rush around, he said, "Like Detective Cutie?"

His nickname for Gage was starting to grow on me so I let it go, but snooping wasn't a nice description. "Yes, and it's investigating. I can't help that I found the poor man and feel compelled to help find whoever attacked him. It was just awful. All that blood frozen on the ice." An involuntary shudder raced through me. "Once I discovered he didn't have a pulse, I couldn't leave him so I sat on the ice while waiting for Gage. I can't remember the last time I felt so helpless."

I set Milo's breakfast on the floor near his water bowl and he dove in like he hadn't eaten in a week. Chuckling, I put water on the stove to boil my cereal. There were many everyday tasks I still liked to do without the help of magic. When I mentioned it to Nikki, she laughed, telling me magic was the best way to live, but being engaged to a non-magical person, I thought it would be better if I could have a toe in both worlds.

Milo was wiping his face with his paws like he did after every meal and grumbled, "What's our first step?"

I flashed him a grin. "You're going to help me?"

He tipped his head. "Consider it my Christmas gift to you. I've decided to skip the shopping and wrapping craziness this year."

Popping my hand on my hip, I said, "Since when do you shop for holiday gifts?"

Padding across the kitchen, he easily jumped onto the chair next to where I would sit. Turning around, he lay down and got comfortable, resting his chin on his paws as he faced my clue board. "There's always a first time."

He flashed me a wide-eyed look and then a slow, lazy wink. "We need to talk about this board. There isn't much to go on yet."

I stirred the oatmeal into the boiling water and turned the burner off so it could finish cooking and as an afterthought, I pointed to the lid on the counter and directed it to the stove. Pleased I could cover the pot with magic, I turned back to the board. "I'm going to start by researching Archie's date, Noelle Webber. They met a couple of weeks ago when they were both working in the same area. He mentioned which company she worked at so finding her home address should be easy. I could run over to Robin's Pointe to see how she's doing."

"Don't you think it's a little odd that a mailman and a delivery driver would show up at precisely the same time at the same house? I mean, what are the odds?"

I quirked a brow and glanced in his direction. "Cynical?"

"No, I'm the practical one in our relationship. You get that lovestruck look every time Gage is around, even before you got the courage to profess your true feelings. Now you think everyone has to have these wonderful love stories. But seriously, Lily, consider it. How many times do you think delivery drivers just happen to bump into one another?"

As much as I didn't want to admit it before coffee, Milo had a point. It was like catching a lobster without bait and I should know since I'd spent just one summer on my uncle Nate's fishing boat. I didn't get asked back for another season after I habitually put traps in the water without any. I poured my coffee and scooped up the oatmeal, adding a healthy spoonful of brown sugar and a sliced banana on top before sitting down.

"Why would Noelle potentially"—I held up a hand so Milo wouldn't interrupt me— "want to bump into Archie? He was a quiet, lonely mailman from a tiny town. It's not like he was an international spy with secrets that he could pass along to make a quick buck."

He shook his head. "My dear witch, have you learned nothing in these last months? A librarian was extorting money out of good people in this town, a real estate agent was getting kickbacks. Do I need to continue?"

"I guess you never do *really* know a person," I said, adding extra emphasis on the word *really* which supported my point about the cases he had brought up. I thought I knew Flora and as far as Teddy Roberts went, well, he had always been a little smarmy. I just hadn't realized how much.

I slid my laptop over in front of me and pushed my now-empty bowl aside. Milo stretched up and glanced my way before licking the remnants of oatmeal from the bowl. It was fine since the bowl would go in the dishwasher anyway. "You know that habit might have to change once Gage and I get married." I held up my left hand to admire my stunning engagement ring. It had been almost two months since he asked me to marry him and I still had to pinch myself that it had really happened.

"I was here first so he'll just have to deal with my"—he paused for dramatic effect—"idiosyncrasies."

"True, but he has a one-hundred-pound lap dog who might challenge you to leftovers."

Milo drew back, his voice now haughty. "I was here first."

He hopped down and stalked from the room. It was hard not to laugh and a muffled, "I can hear you," reached me. I smothered the sounds until I stopped. Dang, I loved that fur ball.

With my laptop and search engine open, I typed in Noelle Webber, Robin's Pointe, and clicked enter. No search results. Maybe I had spelled her name wrong. But I tried a few combinations of her first and last name without success. "Hmm. Maybe I'll see if the delivery company is located nearby."

I entered the company's name and the typical ones popped up including We DOT and there was a website. I clicked over to that and there was an exterior shot of the building. In the middle of the webpage, it announced:

We DOT

WE DELIVER ON TIME:

GUARANTEED!

In looking over the pictures of happy employees working, I found Noelle Webber. Bingo. This was my starting point. I took a picture of the address on my cell phone and called out to Milo, "Are you catching a ride with me to the bookstore this morning or will you meet me there?" I had to wait a couple of minutes to give him time to make up his mind and then slink into the kitchen. With it being so cold and snowy out, I knew what his answer would be, but I preferred to let him tell me. It kept the lines of communication open between us which was important, especially when he was sulking.

Out of the corner of my eye, I could see his gray head peek around the arch of the hallway. In a gruff voice, he said, "I call shotgun."

I didn't bother to point out that he was the only other being that would be in the car. "Excellent." I closed the laptop and slipped it into my bag. With a flick of my wrist, the dirty dishes appeared in the sink. "Ready?" I crossed to the coat rack and was slipping on my jacket when I heard Milo say, half under his breath, "Where you go I will always follow. You are my favorite witch."

I smiled to myself. It didn't matter if this witch and familiar bickered from time to time. There was an unbreakable bond between us.

• • •

We arrived at The Cozy Nook just before eight. Walking from the back entrance through the store, I looked out the window and could see yellow crime scene tape fluttering in the cold morning breeze. It was devoid of people at this hour which was a bonus since I wanted to zip over to take another look. "Milo, I'll be right back."

As I magically flipped the lock with a tiny finger movement, I noticed Milo had settled onto the window seat. He was going to observe from the warmth and comfort of the store. I crossed the brick sidewalk, taking care not to slip on the few icy spots, and hurried to the edge of the yellow tape. It was encompassing the outer edge of the ice. I looked to where I had found Archie and the ice was back to its normal bluish-white color. I exhaled a sigh of relief. No one would have the blood stain as a memory of this happy time of year. I moved in the direction of the entrance and the cookie and cocoa stands. I still found it odd that Archie met someone here so late at night. And was the light left on as a beacon to draw someone in to investigate so an unsuspecting child wouldn't have discovered the scene first?

My footsteps crunched on the crust of the snow as I grew closer to the food stands. A snip of color stuck to the counter caught my eye. Tipping my head and withdrawing my cell phone from my jacket, I took a few pictures. It was a small scrap of green fabric with part of the LL Bean logo and the yellow tape had been ripped down in this section. Who had been here after the police left? Glancing around, I wondered if that person was still lurking. But the birds were quiet and the square was silent. I was confident I was alone.

I was ready to tap the speed dial button for Gage when I decided to finish walking the perimeter. Maybe I'd come up with something else that had happened after everyone had left. I continued around the corner and now I was on the back side of the bright-green wooden benches where skaters could change from boots to skates, but I didn't see anything out of the ordinary. Moving slowly, I was in line with the town hall to my left, and Bee Bee's Boutique was across the street, but it was dark as were the other storefronts. I looked in the direction of The Sweet Spot, where William would be stirring up wonderful cakes, cookies, and, with any luck my favorite pecan cinnamon rolls. First, I needed to finish my surveillance and call Gage about the scrap of the jacket and crime scene tape being disturbed.

When I finished my walk, I called Gage and as usual, he picked up on the first ring. "Hey, Lily, are you at the store already?"

I didn't want to make him worry. "I was but then I decided to come over to the rink and just take another look. You need to come down here. Maybe even send Sharon or Mac. Someone was here after you left."

"Why do you say that?" I could hear the concern laced in his voice.

"Near the food stands there is a rip from a

jacket and the yellow tape has been taken down. You need to see this and I promise I didn't touch a thing." I wanted to add even though I have latex gloves and was more than capable of looking closer, I left it all just as I found it.

"I'm just leaving home, but I'll call the team and let them know. Someone will be there in a flash and if anyone approaches you, don't engage."

"What? Like start questioning them why they're at the scene of a crime or if they did it?" I could picture Gage shaking his head, exasperated that I would even joke about doing something like that because in reality, we both knew I would. "I'll be careful." Which was the best I could do given the circumstances and I also could wrap a protection spell around me if I got really freaked out.

After he disconnected, I realized I should have asked him about Noelle Webber. Had Archie taken her home and then come back? I could ask when he arrived. Until then, I stood close to where the fabric clung to a jagged corner of the stand and I started to think about who wore a bright-green jacket in this particular shade.

Something was bugging me about this part of the rink, and as I kept looking around, it dawned on me, there were no boot or shoe prints but there were slashes like blades from skates. This made sense since last night people were changing shoes at the benches and then walking over this shortcut to enter the ice. But if someone had gained access to the area via this location, they must have been wearing skates and who would take the chance to get caught wearing those? You certainly couldn't run from the cops wearing ice skates no matter how sure-footed you were. They had to have taken another way in. I made another quick loop around the rink and came back to where I started but other than my footsteps hugging the rink, there were no other telltale signs anyone had been there. By the time I got back to where the tape was fluttering in the breeze, Gage and Dax were jogging through the park in my direction. I waved to them. When they got to where I was, Gage kissed my cheek and Dax said, "Morning, Lily."

"Hey, Dax. You look tired."

He nodded. "I just got back from Robin's Pointe," and he clamped his mouth shut.

"Does that mean you talked with Noelle?" I looked from him to Gage, but neither of them answered me. "You know I'm going to find out so why don't you just tell me." I arched a brow in a gesture that Gage should recognize. If they didn't start talking, I would be going from here to Robin's Pointe, or even better, my next stop would be We DOT.

Chapter 5
Lily

When neither Gage nor Dax spoke, I said, "Never mind." I turned on my heel and stalked away.

"Lily. Wait," Gage called after me and I could feel the smile spread across my face. A change of heart. Surpress the grin, I turned and hoped I was giving him a neutral look—at least I was doing my best. He was crossing the town square to where I stood.

"Will you show us what you found?"

Frustration bubbled up inside and I rolled my eyes. Pointing to where the tape wafted on the wind, I said, "Right there, and the cloth is stuck to the wood counter."

I kept my shoulders from drooping and crossed the street to my shop. Only after I was inside with my coat off did I walk to the window seat and plop down. "Milo, you're never going to guess what happened."

He opened one eye as I stroked the top of his head between his ears. "Do tell."

I kept one eye on what was happening across the street as I told him about the tattered piece of cloth and the crime scene tape. "It's obvious someone came back, and when I asked the guys about why Dax had gone to Robin's Pointe, they clammed up. I tell you, maybe I should think about not oversharing what I learn and let them catch up to me."

Milo rolled onto his side and I scratched his belly. "That's not a good idea going off and then not sharing important information with the police. They can charge you with obstruction of justice, and even if Gage wouldn't, Dax might if he thought it would keep you safe."

I sighed. He did have a good point. I know how protective they both were of me. Dax had grown into being like the annoying brother I always wanted but never had. I got why he might take drastic measures. But something had happened with Noelle and if Dax had gone to the next town over, he must have questioned her. "Are you up for a ride before we open the store?"

He flicked his tail. "Call Mimi and see if she'll cover the shop. You don't want to miss any potential customers this close to Christmas. And while we're out and about, maybe consider stopping by the post office and talking to Etta; she's still the postmaster. I'll bet she has some information on Archie that no one else has."

"Right. His boss would know if he had a run-in with anyone and also what his route was. We could drive it to see where he might have met Noelle. But that is all after we talk to her. She knows things that we don't."

I got up and called my aunt. She quickly agreed to cover the store for me for as long as necessary which worked out perfectly given how much I needed to pack into one trip. We'd see Noelle, We DOT, and Etta at the post office and given a little bit of luck, Archie's route around Pembroke Cove.

Aunt Mimi breezed in the front door, waving to Nate as he pulled away from the curb. "Good morning, Lily." She paused to give Milo a treat. I hoped someday I'd be like the petite dynamo with long gray hair and sable-brown eyes that sparkled with mischief. "Where are you and Milo off to this morning?"

"Did you hear the news about Archie Dane?"

She narrowed her eyes. "Please don't tell me what I think you are..."

"He was killed late last night at the ice rink."

My aunt's eyes grew wide as they met mine. Her voice laced with concern softened,

"Please don't tell me you were the one to find him."

"Gage drove me home after we left the skating rink and my car was behind the store. I wanted to get in here early and didn't want to have Gage come pick me up. When he turned off to go to his house, I drove past the rink on my way home, and that's when I noticed the light was on at the cocoa stand. I thought Regan had forgotten. It would only take a minute to shut it off but once I got to the stand, I noticed a person on the ice. But it was too late; he was already dead."

She wrapped her arms around me and held me close. It felt good to talk about it again just to replay it in my mind to see if I had missed anything important.

"I'm sorry this happened to you again. And don't take this the wrong way, but I'm glad he was found before this morning. That would have been just awful if a child had stumbled upon the scene."

She continued to hold me and murmur

soothing, magical words and the tension in my body eased away. As I relaxed, she stepped back and held my gaze. "Do you feel better?"

I kissed her cheek. "What would I do without you?"

"You don't have to; longevity is in our genes." She placed a hand on my cheek. "You're going in search of answers. Is Nikki going with you?"

"No. Milo is going. There's nothing to worry about. I'm going to chat with Archie's date from last night, the delivery company the woman works for, and then swing by the post office."

With a thoughtful nod, she said, "Close your eyes."

I did as she asked and I felt her hands on my shoulders. "Enhance this young witch's protection spell from the moment I ring the bell. For this I wish, so shall it be."

The door opened and the bell jingled.

She kissed my cheek and whispered in my ear, "Perfect timing."

Gage and Dax came inside and I looked out the window. Mac and Peabody were near the cocoa stand.

"Are they finding anything else?" I didn't expect Gage would tell me, but it didn't hurt to ask.

He held out a bag that bore The Sweet Spot's logo and Dax held out a drink tray with four cups. He gave me a crooked smile and Aunt Mimi a wink. In his charming, slow Southern drawl he said, "Peace offering?"

"Dax." Aunt Mimi gestured to the back room. "Why don't we get the sweets arranged on a plate and warm the coffee." He took the bag from Gage and followed her as if she were the Pied Piper.

Flashing Gage a grin, she said, "Good luck."

When they were out of earshot, he asked, "Am I going to need it?"

"No. But I would like to know what you were holding back earlier." I nodded to the town square. "I called you as soon as I saw there had been a disturbance and I know Dax talked with Noelle Webber, so what's the big deal?"

He pointed to our favorite wingback chairs that were placed with an excellent view of the street and the square. "Can we sit for a minute?"

I glanced at the back room where my aunt and Dax were hiding. "Of course." I sat down in what I considered my chair and Gage sat next to me. Taking my hand in his, he said, "I'm sorry I can't share every detail of an ongoing investigation with you. It's not that I don't trust you, but I want to keep you out of the fray." He squeezed my hand gently. "You have to admit trouble has a way of finding you."

I wasn't going to agree with that statement. "If you keep me in the dark, that means we're wasting time finding out who did this."

"We"—he pointed to me and then him— "don't need to follow the clues and discover the truth." He pointed to where Dax was holed up. "He and I need to follow them where they lead."

"But you've always said I'm good at puzzles and look at how much help I was the last few times there has been a serious situation in town." I knew he couldn't deny that it was information I uncovered that led to a satisfying conclusion and justice for each of the victims.

"And each time you followed the clues, what happened to you?"

I waved a hand in the air, pushing off the reminders that I had a couple of close calls. "That was nothing. Besides, every day my magic is getting stronger and I'm better able to defend myself should the need arise."

"That's the point, sweetheart. I don't want you to have to. Your magic should be helping you get kittens down from trees or helping a mermaid in distress in the harbor, or maybe even catching the biggest fish when we go out on the boat this summer. But tracking down clues that lead to a murderer is something I'd rather you leave to me."

"I'm better at solving puzzles and you can't deny that fact. In addition, these are nothing more than elaborate, and sometimes a tad more dangerous, brain twisters." I gave him a poke in the chest to emphasize my point. "I'm going to ask questions so it's in your best interest to share what you know so you don't have to worry as much about me." I made an X over my heart. "I cross my heart I'll be super careful and I'm taking Milo with me."

He frowned. "So despite what I've said, you're still determined to question people whom you don't know?"

"Only one or two are unknown, the rest I know." I gave him a comical grin in hopes it would get him to loosen up. "Come on, you know the information I uncover is always valuable to your investigation."

Dax and Aunt Mimi came back and he was carrying a tray of coffee mugs and a platter of cinnamon buns and scones. "Gage, she's right. We should tell her at least some of what we've discovered. There is nothing you can say that will dissuade her from going off on her own."

Aunt Mimi nodded. "She has a good arsenal of spells and this morning I boosted her self-protection spell to give it more power."

I gave him a triumphant grin. "What do you say? Are you going to tell me what Dax was doing in Robin's Pointe today?"

Gage shook his head. "I'm going on record saying I don't think you should go off on your own or with just Milo as a backup. Why can't Nikki ride along?"

Milo slunk over and shot an annoyed look at Gage as he mumbled, "If the non-magical human was able to understand me, he'd know how much trouble a handsome, twelve-pound bundle of fur could be. And did I hear Gage say I was *just* a backup? Like I'm not capable of helping you? Is he forgetting how we worked together at the library to get you out of there before he showed up?"

He jumped onto my lap and glared at Gage while Dax smothered a laugh and Aunt Mimi did her best to keep her face neutral. I ran a hand down Milo's back. "Nikki has a business that is very busy this time of year and I can't ask her to leave it every time I get an idea that needs to be followed up on."

His eyebrow shot up but he didn't ask what my familiar had said. Instead, his eyes shifted to my aunt. I knew what he was thinking before he even put that thought into words.

"This is different. I ran this store for many years and when I sold the business to Lily, we had an agreement that I would be happy to fill in as needed." She snapped her head in a sharp nod. "This is one of those times so, Detective Erikson, the way I see it, you can do one of two things. Give Lily something to go on..." She held up her hand, stopping Gage before he could even think of interrupting her. "Or let her go off and hunt down all the information she wants and maybe waste time doing so."

Gage looked at Dax. "You're not saying much."

He didn't bother to smother his laugh this time. "Buddy, we have no choice but to bring Lily and Mimi in on what little we know. Besides, it's not like Lily hasn't seen most of everything and if it wasn't for her checking things out this morning, we wouldn't have the new clue."

The look on Gage's face told me he was beginning to come around to the idea of sharing information.

"I'm not thrilled but I see value in what Dax and Mimi have said." He gave Dax a nod. "Go ahead and tell her about Noelle."

He pulled up two small side chairs for my aunt and himself and they sat down. I took a mug of coffee to perk up my brain cells and with it hovering near my lips, I waited before taking that first sip.

"Last night, as we were leaving the scene, Gage and I decided to walk around looking for Archie's Jeep."

"And you found it?"

"We did. It was near the town hall on the side of the road. As we approached it, we could see someone inside, but they didn't respond when we called out. As I opened the door, Noelle fell out from the driver's side."

"What? She was there the entire time?" I

felt the color drain from my face as another more sinister idea took root. "Wait, was she hurt or worse?"

"No, she was sound asleep. We told her the news and questioned her at the station, and then I drove her home. On the ride she didn't have much to say. She seemed to be in shock or doing a great job acting like she was. Gage said they hadn't been dating long so her reaction wasn't over the top, so that tracked."

Aunt Mimi asked, "What do you mean by that?"

"There are two ends of the spectrum when there is an unexpected death of someone close to you. Either the person is inconsolable or almost relieved. Noelle wasn't either. She was quiet."

"Do you think she was really sleeping?" I asked.

"She didn't have any visible blood on her hands or clothes and when Gage was asking her questions, I did a little spell I worked up to double check. If I had discovered any blood, he would have run through the standard procedure to log that information as evidence."

Nodding, I said, "So either she wasn't that attached to Archie and she really did fall asleep or she's the murderer." And I intended to find out which.

Chapter 6
Gage

I watched Lily's face as Dax relayed the evidence about Noelle Webber. She was absorbing the information and I wondered as fast she stored it to be retrieved at a later date, would it be as detailed? She was razor sharp. Although I continued to try to discourage her from following the clues, I was very proud of her, too. Brilliant didn't even come close to how she looked at puzzles and figured things out.

Dax said, "When we got to Noelle's apartment, she asked me if I wanted to come in for coffee. I took this as an opportunity to survey her living space. At this point, I had no reason to doubt she was waiting in the truck and fell asleep as she said, but without anyone to vouch for her, it's still an open question."

"What was her place like?" Lily was picking at a pecan cinnamon bun and drinking coffee, but her focus was entirely on Dax.

"Pretty messy. Stacks of newspapers and magazines on the tabletops. I could see into the kitchen and it didn't look like she was any tidier in there. It wasn't hard to miss, her sink was overflowing with dirty dishes."

Mimi said, "That's not a crime. It's unsanitary but lots of people live like that."

"True. But when I looked at her hair and makeup, it was flawless. I expected it to carry over into her home too." Dax grabbed a scone, broke it in half, and then nicked off a small piece and offered it to Milo, who made it disappear like magic.

That made me wonder, was that my way into Milo's good graces, through treats? I know my rescue dog, Brutus, would do anything for food which is why he weighed over one hundred pounds and was still growing girth wise. Dax continued to tell Lily that although the apartment was messy, he didn't notice any signs of Archie having been at the house.

I watched as a thoughtful gaze filled her beautiful face. "It was a new relationship. He would still be coming over when invited, maybe sharing a meal, not leaving personal belongings strewn about." She tapped a finger to her lips. "Why was she asleep in his Jeep?"

Dax smiled. My Lily never missed a trick. He had skirted around that conversation and away from why Noelle was in the truck and Lily twirled it right back. "According to Noelle, Archie was driving her home around nine o'clock and he got a call. Which much to her annoyance, he answered. After a few *rights* and *okays*, he said they needed to run back to the skating rink and it would only take a minute. A friend needed his help and it couldn't wait."

Lily said, "Interesting. They stayed until

the end which means the rink should have been closed down by the time they got back. If that's true, why park closer to the town hall than the rink? When I pulled up after noticing the lights, I parked right next to the entrance."

"Dear, did you happen to see any other cars when you got out?" Mimi was also captivated by the unfolding information. Like aunt, like niece.

Lily closed her eyes as if replaying the scene and shook her head. "No. I didn't look around. It was cold and I just wanted to shut down the lights and get home. But I think I would have noticed if there was a vehicle parked on the street." She looked at Dax. "That puts Archie back at the town square roughly, nine-thirty?"

"Noelle said she didn't look at the time but that's a good guesstimate."

"Alright then, Archie is meeting Mr. X near the rink and Noelle waits for him. But I thought you said she fell asleep. If you're just waiting for a person doing a quick errand, would you just nod off?" Her lips pursed and she said, "Nope. Not buying that since you said she fell out of the Jeep when you opened the door. Are you sure she was actually sleeping or faking it?"

"Whoa, Lily." I was surprised at her pointing an accusing finger at Noelle. I had my suspicions too, but she had seemed to be truthful when we questioned her. For now, I would scrutinize everyone who had a possible motive.

She tipped her head in my direction and said, "I know that you are thinking the exact same way. And we don't know this person. We met her for all of a minute or two last night. Archie was a sweet, nerdy kind of a guy and she was waiting in the Jeep and fell asleep? That takes some time. I'd be one of two things if you went to meet someone—either anxious since you were only going to be gone a couple of minutes or mad as heck. In either situation, I'd come looking for you."

And that was exactly the conclusion I had

drawn and Dax was nodding as that was his too. "Why do you think she is claiming to have been sleeping?"

Lily said, "I don't know but I'll let you know after I talk to her." Milo hopped onto her lap and gave me a hard, unblinking stare as if saying he agreed with her. "And don't even think of telling me that I shouldn't. If I was taking bets, I would say she'll tell me more than she told Dax. People get nervous around a police officer even if they have nothing to hide."

"What if you ask Nate to drive with you to Robin's Pointe?"

Crossing her arms over her midsection, she glared at me and that was never a good sign. "Gage Erikson. Are you implying that I'm not capable of taking care of myself and Milo? We're not close to solving the case so there's no reason for anyone to want to harm me. Whoever did this knows there is nothing at this point to tie them back to the rink last night. Unless you've found something else you're not telling me."

I looked away, not wanting to wilt under her withering gaze. But she might as well know about the mailbag. "We did find one thing at the rink after you left. A sack of mail."

Her eyes lit up. "Any chance it was behind the cocoa stand? When I was going to turn the lights off, I tripped over something but noticed Archie lying on the ice and promptly forgot about it."

"Yes. Any ideas why it might have been there?"

"You should ask Regan. If Archie, Ellen, or Chet asked to store it back there, she'd know." She scrunched up her face and said more to herself than us, "But that makes no sense. If it was Archie's, he had gotten off work and went to pick up Noelle. He wouldn't have been carrying a mailbag around. And it's negligent to think he'd have mail outside his truck or the post office itself. Besides, he was a stickler for following the rules." She chewed her lower lip. "But it's another thread to tug."

She got up from the chair and picked up a

pad and pen and began to write something down. When she was done, she looked at Dax, Mimi, and me and grinned. "I had to get that all down so I can transfer it to my clue board when I get home tonight." With a tap on the arm of my chair, she said, "Don't you gentlemen have someplace you need to be, people to talk to, like Regan?"

Now she was getting sassy and it was darn cute. "Are you kicking us out?"

With a wink at Mimi, Lily said, "You can stay. I'm sure my aunt can find something for you to do since I am leaving. Which means coffee time is officially over."

I glanced at Dax and grinned. "Guess that is our cue to get back to work." And I wasn't about to admit that our first stop was Robin's Café. We needed to have a conversation with Regan about that mailbag which included if she left the lights on. At this point I was sure the entire town knew bits and pieces of what had happened.

I stood up and swept Lily into my arms.

Holding her close, I said, "Please be careful and if anything makes the hair on the back of your neck stand up, listen to that signal and get back in your car and call me."

She tipped her head back and smiled. "Does that mean you'll be my knight on a white horse and rescue me?"

I leaned into her. "More like a guy driving a red pickup. But yes, I will always come to your rescue."

She pecked my lips. "Right back at ya, Detective."

Milo grumbled and she smiled again. "And Milo says he'd even think about lending a paw too."

Dax chuckled and Mimi grinned. I had a feeling Milo said more than he'd help out. But I was going to let that go. I made a mental note to talk with my mom and see if there was any way I could learn to speak familiar. Otherwise, I had a strong suspicion I was going to be the butt of a few jokes in the years ahead.

The door opened and the bell above the

door jangled. Fred Wickshire, owner of The Clam Bake, came in and looked at our little group. "Good morning, Lily. Are you open?"

Mimi rose gracefully from her chair and said, "Hello, Fred. Doing a little Christmas shopping?"

"Yes, but if you're busy, I can come back."

She slipped her arm through the crook of his, exclaiming, "Nonsense. Everyone is just leaving so we'll have plenty of quiet to get your shopping done." She gave us a pointed look and jerked her head toward the street as if telling us to get going.

I gave Fred a nod. "Good to see you."

"Likewise, Gage. Dax." And his face softened when he turned to Lily. "I haven't seen you at the restaurant lately."

"That's sweet that you noticed, Fred. It's been busy with the holidays, but Gage and I will come by very soon."

"I can do a lovely wedding reception." He gave us both a sly wink.

I could feel the color rise in my cheeks. As

much as I'd love to rush down the aisle and marry Lily, we both wanted to take our time. "Thanks, Fred. We'll certainly keep that in mind but we haven't even set a date yet."

I looked at Mimi and hoped she would divert his attention away from us and back on his shopping trip.

"Now, Fred, who is on your list this year so we can find suitable gifts for everyone?"

He withdrew a paper from his pocket and handed it to her. She smiled and said, "This is quite a few people, but trust me, we'll get this done for you. I'll even make sure all the gifts are wrapped and I can drop them by the restaurant later today." She escorted him down the mystery aisle and out of sight.

I gave Lily a kiss. "Remember, call if you need me."

She gave me a playful push toward the door. "Go, Milo and I will be fine." When I still didn't move, she said, "Dax, please help me get this big lug out the door. Otherwise, I'll never get back to the shop today."

"Sure thing, Lily."

"I'm going, but dinner tonight?"

"You can cook and let's have the gang over and we can talk about the case."

It wasn't exactly what I had in mind, but bringing Nikki and Steve into the party would make it easier to let them know what was going on. Maybe Nikki would have some time to be Watson to Lily's Sherlock. "I'll let Peabody and Mac know too in case they want to come over."

"Alright." She opened the door and with a hand on her hip, she said in a light teasing voice, "Be safe out there today."

I tweaked her nose. "Same for you, just double."

She closed the door with me on the outside, all the while laughing. I knew resorting to something we said to each other in high school might be juvenile, but it slipped out of my mouth.

"You know, you're either going to have to come to terms with Lily helping us or you'll drive yourself buggy." Dax headed in the direction of the café.

Falling in step beside him, I asked, "If she was your fiancée, how would you handle it?"

"Trust her. She's smart, a skilled witch, and Milo will be an extra set of eyes. I know you don't believe this, but her familiar is more than just a cat. He guides her and pushes her to become stronger every day. It's his role to keep her safe while she's new to witchcraft and as she gets older and more experienced, their bond will continue to deepen."

We were close to the café when I stopped walking. "Why don't you have a familiar? I thought all witches did."

"Most do but like the woman I'm waiting for, I'm also prepared for the day I discover my familiar. And don't forget I grew up very different from Lily. In our household, magic was embraced. She grew up without it since her father made the choice to live as a non-magical like Lily's mom."

Reed and Mindy Michaels had chosen to

live on the outskirts of Pembroke Cove. When Lily came back a few years ago, she started to work with Mimi at the bookstore. Her plan had been to take it over when Mimi was ready to retire.

"When we have kids, I want them to grow up like I did, experiencing the magic that is all around you. My mom is a witch and my dad isn't, but that didn't stop them from sharing every nuance of her craft with me."

A customer came out of the café and held the door for us, cutting short my ramblings.

"Come on, let's talk to Regan and see if she can fill us in on the mailbag."

I let Dax go ahead of me. "Be prepared to answer a ton of questions. To get information, we'll have to give some up."

He gave me a look as if I was crazy. "Small towns. An equal opportunity grapevine is always in play. If we do this correctly, we can flush out more leads and information than we give."

The door closed behind me and Dax said,

"I'm following your lead and any information you decide to share is your choice. Me, I'm doing it the way I know how. Asking questions and not answering any."

I clapped my hand on his shoulder. "Let me show you how to navigate small-town investigating. Someday you might be flying solo and need these skills."

Dax chuckled. "Unlikely."

Chapter 7
Lily

I drove down the main street in Robin's Pointe. The town was charming and decorated for the holidays with wreaths in the storefront windows. Small Christmas trees with brightly colored lights flanked each door, and vibrant red bows were attached to the benches every ten feet, which lined the sidewalks. I had passed Robin's Point Inn on the way into town and that was festive too. The widow walk was draped with garland and bows. Something about that house drew me in. There had been a small sign advertising tea and sweets. Maybe I'd swing by and have a cup with the owner. With any luck, she might know Noelle Webber and be able to give me some insight.

At the end of the street on the left side was the building I had been looking for: We DOT. There were two small vans parked out front that bore the same logo. "Milo, we found the right place."

He arched his back and stretched from his lounging position in the passenger seat. "That was quick." Putting his front paws on the dashboard, he surveyed the parking area. "Looks like an average non-magical place."

I laughed. "What did you expect it to look like, Santa's workshop?"

He went back to a sitting position and gave me a side-eye. "No decorations for starters. Would it have killed them to hang a wreath on the front door or a small tree on the sidewalk?"

I hated to remind him, but I didn't like that he was passing judgment on whoever owned this business. "Not everyone celebrates the holidays."

He resumed his earlier position, standing on his back legs, and took another look around. "Lily, the building is dull tan, with a brown door and those weird blinds in the window. Look, even one side is half-up or half-down; it's hard to say. There's no curb appeal, but if you look at the other storefronts, they're bursting with holiday cheer. Would you want to come to this building every day for work?"

"Point taken but we're not working here. We're just stopping in to ask a few questions." I pushed open the driver's door and got out. "Are you staying here?"

"Yup. I'm the lookout."

Knowing he was serious, I didn't laugh. "How will I know if something's wrong?"

With a wave of his paw, he said, "Don't worry. I have ways. Remember when I helped you sneak out of the library?"

I couldn't help it. The grin spread across my face as he brought up the library incident again. "And I had to walk home without shoes."

Milo nodded. "Good times. Now go so we can knock one stop off your list."

Before I closed the door, I grabbed a warm, fuzzy throw blanket and tucked it around him. "In case you get chilled." He purred his thanks, then turned around three times before he snuggled in.

I closed the door behind me and hurried up the freshly shoveled walkway. They might have cockeyed blinds, but someone had done a good job of clearing the walk and gave it a liberal amount of salt. On the door was a sign with business hours. I eased it open. Somewhere in the back a buzzer announced my arrival.

A muffled "Be right there" drifted from the recesses of the back room. I looked around the sparsely furnished office. There was a plywood counter that had been painted tan, a matching tan carpet that was covered with stains and a very uncomfortable-looking chair next to a scarred wooden table. All in all, it was pretty shabby and the only item in the room that looked professional was the desktop computer in front of me.

A door burst open and I was surprised to see Noelle standing in front of me. She was wearing a nondescript long-sleeved tan shirt with the company logo over the left pocket and jeans. This morning her hair was pulled back in a high ponytail, but I could have sworn her eyes were blue. Now they were bright green, and wasn't her hair brown last night? Contacts maybe, but it didn't explain the hair. "Lily, this is a surprise." Confusion filled her face and she looked around the lobby, I assume to see if I was alone.

"Hi, Noelle. I was hoping I would find you here." And I was. However, I hadn't expected to see her at her job, but rather in her apartment, processing the news that her new boyfriend was dead.

"Did you want to ship a package?"

It was obvious I wasn't holding a box or bag, but I went along with answering her question.

"No, I wanted to check to see how you were doing. Detectives Gage Erikson and Dax Peters told me about last night. I wanted to express how sorry I was." I figured tossing in the cop angle might be helpful in getting her to talk.

She sniffed but there were no tears in the corners of her bright, clear eyes. In fact, there was no sign of crying at all. "Thank you. But we hadn't been dating that long so it wasn't like I was overly attached."

I took a step back. That sounded harsh. "But to be killed mere yards from where you were sitting has to be upsetting."

Her face paled. "I thought he fell and hit his head on the ice. I had no idea." A look of horror passed over her face. "Do you think the person he was meeting meant to hurt him?"

Now there was emotion. Real or fake was the only question. "It's possible. Did you see or hear anything or anyone before you fell asleep in the Jeep?" I needed her to know that I knew all about last night, well to a certain degree.

"No. Archie left the Jeep running to keep

the heater on for me. I was chilled to the bone after skating, and he had been so sweet and bought me a cocoa for the ride home. He told me to wait for him and I tuned the radio to Christmas music. After a few minutes, I couldn't keep my eyes open. The next thing I knew I was falling out of the vehicle and that cop with the soothing, Southern drawl, he caught me."

"Dax Peters."

"Yeah, that's the one." Her shoulders drooped. "And all that time Archie was lying on the hard, freezing-cold ice." She looked up and her eyes had grown wider but was it from sadness? "Do you think it hurt?"

"When he fell?" I nodded. "I'm sure it did in that instant, but I'd like to think that he slipped away and didn't feel pain."

The edges of her lips turned down. "Who's going to deliver the mail?"

I nearly did a double-take. What was the big deal about the mail? As much as I wanted to ask her, I figured that should be something

Gage checked out. "I wonder if I can ask you another question that doesn't have anything to do with Archie."

"Yeah, go for it." She leaned on the counter as if she didn't have a care in the world.

"Do you wear contacts?"

She smiled. "I have every color they make." Batting her eyelashes, she said, "What do you think? The green ones are my favorite but when I met Archie, I had the blue ones in and he mentioned how much he loved my blue eyes so when we went out, I'd wear those. And before you ask, I have wigs too. I hate to get tied into just one look."

And a great way to appear to be someone else was the first thing that popped into my mind. "Well, this combination gives you the look of an Irish lass."

She beamed. "Thank you. That's the nicest thing anyone has said to me in a long time."

I thanked her for talking with me and before I got out the door, she said, "Any idea when I can get my other skate back? They were borrowed and I need to return them."

I froze my hand on the door pull. I never mentioned finding her skate. I caught her studying me intently. "Um. You'll need to check with Detective Erikson."

"Or that other cute detective might know." I was sure my expression was shocked as she said, "Hey, my date died, but I can still think a guy is cute. There's no crime in that, is there?"

Between mentioning the skate and re-marking on Dax, Noelle Webber just moved to the top of my suspect list. "Where did you say you met Archie?"

Her smile became wistful. "It was romantic. We were both delivering packages to this business in Pembroke Cove and I dropped my box and Archie picked it up for me."

"And where was that?"

"Robin's Café. I deliver there every other week."

I didn't have anything else to say so I thanked her for talking with me and hurried back to my Mini Cooper. Milo popped his head up from the cozy blanket on the seat after enjoying his nap as soon as I got in and started the car.

"How did it go?"

I shivered. "I have no idea what Archie saw in Noelle because so far, she is my only suspect. My working theory is that they got into an argument, she threw the skate at him, and then pushed him back and went to the Jeep to wait, got tired, and fell asleep."

"Don't you think that's just a little too convenient?"

I clutched the steering wheel and stared at the nondescript building in front of us. "Maybe but she either did it or knows who and why actually harmed Archie. Rest assured, I will find out."

Backing out of my parking place, Milo asked, "Where to next?"

"I need a pick-me-up and we're going to stop and have tea at a charming inn on the way out of town."

Milo grumbled, "Hopefully familiars are welcome."

I scratched the top of his head. "If they're not, we won't stay. I'll order it to go." I swear he had never purred louder when I said that.

I pulled into the circular driveway and upon a closer look the inn was spectacular. It was three stories high with a sweeping porch. Much to Milo's happiness, it was decorated with a Christmas tree on either side of the front door, garland swept along the porch roof, and a wreath on every window. There were even twinkle lights intertwined into the garland.

He was standing on his back legs as we came to a stop. "Now, these people know how to keep Christmas. I wonder if the inside looks as nice."

"There's only one way to find out. I'll run in and ask if you can come in too."

"Look, there's a cutout of a black cat on the

top of the step. Go see what it says." The excitement in his voice couldn't contain his curiosity and it was sweet at the same time.

I ran lightly up the wide front steps and lifted my hand to knock when the door swung open.

A tall, curvaceous woman stood in the doorway. Her dark hair had ribbons of silver-gray, and it was swept up into a bun. Her eyes were green and reminded me of a cat, and her smile was warm with deep dimples to accentuate it. She was beautiful. "Hello and welcome to the Robin's Pointe Inn. I'm Minerva Robertson."

I placed a hand on my chest and the smile came effortlessly. "Hi. I'm Lily Michaels and I saw your sign for tea. I was hoping you were open today."

She pulled the door wider. "Come in, my dear."

I glanced over my shoulder at my car. "I know this may be an odd request, but would you mind if my cat Milo came inside? It's so cold and..."

"Of course, any cat of yours is welcome here."

"Thank you." I jogged down the stairs and opened the passenger door. "Now be on your best behavior."

Milo gave me a haughty look. "I'm not a barn cat. I do know how to attend tea." With a grace he reserved for important moments, he ascended the steps stopped, and inclined his head to the porch floor. "Thank you, Miss Minerva."

I came up behind him and scooped him into my arms. "Thank you again."

She reached out and scratched his ears. "You're welcome, Milo."

Did my familiar just give her a wink? As we entered the house, Milo and I looked around. It was ornately decorated but tasteful. "Your inn is lovely."

She ushered us into a parlor where a fire was blazing in the fieldstone fireplace. Despite the size of the room, it felt cozy and warm. "Please relax on one of the settees and I'll get tea. Would you like sweets or something more substantial?"

"Whatever isn't any trouble." I gave her a wide smile. Minerva was a lovely hostess.

She inclined her head. "I'll be right back. Make yourself at home."

I chose a damask-covered seat and placed Milo next to me. "This makes up for the lackluster decorations at We DOT, right?"

"Miss Minerva could teach them a thing or two." Milo stretched out so that his side would absorb the maximum amount of warmth from the fire crackling in the grate.

It seemed like seconds when Minerva returned and set the tray on the table in front of me. It was filled with tea sandwiches, cookies, a large floral china teapot, and two delicate matching cups. One of the plates held slivers of smoked salmon.

"May I join you and Milo?"

"Please." I accepted the cup of tea and it smelled vaguely familiar. I smiled. "Is this a blend from MRM Teas?"

"Yes, how did you know?" She stirred a drizzle of honey in her cup and sipped.

"They're my parents, Mindy and Reed Michaels."

"Small world. But tell me, why are you in Robin's Pointe today?" She passed me a plate of sandwiches and I selected a cucumber and smoked salmon and smiled my thanks.

I thought of Noelle and all the unanswered questions I had. "I needed to speak with a woman about a friend of mine who passed away last night. I was hoping she could answer a few questions." I nibbled the sandwich and audibly groaned. "This is delicious."

Beaming, Minerva said, "Thank you. Did you find the answers you were looking for?"

Shaking my head, I said, "Sadly, I have more questions now than answers. But that's only temporary. I love puzzles and at some point, I'll figure it out."

"I'm sure you will." She seemed to be enjoying our visit as the inn was quiet as a church mouse.

"Do you have many guests this time of year?"

"A few. I'm expecting a long-term guest who'll be arriving tomorrow. I'm looking forward to it. He's a writer and has proposed to write a book about my family's history and our charming little town."

"That is exciting." I took an oatmeal cookie from the plate she extended. The moment the cookie hit my taste buds, it was as if a flavor explosion happened. "This is the best cookie I've ever eaten, but please don't tell my best friend. She's a baker and she's great, but this cookie is just... wow."

"Feel free to take a couple with you. Maybe she can replicate them. But I don't share the recipe with anyone outside of the family."

I bobbed my head, understanding that family recipes were part of our heritage. "I'm sure your family must love when you bake."

"I have three nieces who used to spend summers with me and there were always fresh cookies in the jar as well as tart lemonade in the fridge too." A wistful expression flitted over her face. "They're grown now and living their own lives, but I expect they'll be coming back to the Pointe this summer for an extended visit."

"I'm sure you'll treasure every moment." I took another cookie. "These are magical."

Her green eyes grew more intense and her smile put me at ease. "Yes, they are. Now tell me about your visit with Noelle Webber. Maybe I can help."

Chapter 8
Lily

I began to choke on the cookie and sputtered, "How did you know who I came to see?"

Minerva gestured to Milo. "Ask your familiar."

And that's when it dawned on me. She had called Milo by his name from the moment we arrived. "You're a witch."

"Just like you." Laughing softly, she said, "I'm sorry to have caught you off guard. It's not often a young witch stops to visit without wanting something from me other than a cup of tea. There are a few who come hoping I'll share my family's knowledge, but they're looking to take shortcuts with their magic and I won't help them. But you, on the other hand, Lily, are a rare witch indeed. Tell me, is your Aunt Mimi well?"

The surprises just kept coming. "Yes, thank you. How well do you know my aunt?"

She gave what I thought looked like a twist on a royal wave and smiled. "We've been friends for more years than I care to mention. However, enough about me. I want to help. That is if you'd care to talk about today."

It would be good to get some of what was bugging me off my chest. I wasn't sure how productive it would be without divulging information on the case. However, if she knew Noelle Webber at all, I might gain better insight. "Why do you think a person would constantly change their personal appearance like wearing wigs, using colored contacts, that sort of thing?"

"Well, some people are unhappy with how they look. I'm sure some do it for fun, while others have something to hide." She looked at me over the rim of the floral tea cup. "Which one of those scenarios do you believe would apply in this situation?"

"I'd like to think the second since Noelle was taking great pleasure in talking about it, but I'm leaning more toward the third option. And she doesn't seem that broken up that a person died. She was more curious about who was going to take over his mail route. I find that to be cold." I shuddered and set my cup down so I could stand in front of the fire.

"Lily, you're projecting how you would feel if someone in your life had been hurt, but maybe they weren't that connected. Dating yes, but she obviously wasn't feeling that spark."

Looking into the fire, I didn't turn around but said, "How did you know they were dating?" I knew I hadn't mentioned it.

"Oh, that's right. You don't know what kind of a witch I am." Her soft laughter caused me to relax. "Part of my gift is telepathy. I am not trying to invade your thoughts, but your encounter with that woman is rolling off you. I tried to block it, but you seemed like you needed to share."

I could hear as she patted the cushion where I had been sitting. "Please have a seat. I won't invade your privacy again."

"Minerva, I was caught off guard that you could read my mind, not that you did. And maybe it was helpful not to voice every little thing she did that annoyed me. I just looked at her as heartless. How could anyone not be bothered when someone loses their life?"

Her eyes were a softer shade of green now and I could see the empathy there. "I do know her. She moved here about a year ago and I have a fair number of packages delivered, most of which come via We DOT. She is an acquired taste and for the record, I don't know why Archie was attracted to her as he was a quiet man."

"You knew him too?"

She nodded. "I allowed him to surf fish from my beach. It's private and he said he didn't like crowds or fishing in a more public area. It seemed to make sense as fishing is a solitary endeavor. I granted him permission to come over whenever he wanted. Actually, I think it was in my driveway where they first met."

I could feel my face scrunch up. "Archie told me they met on a delivery and Noelle just confirmed the same thing. She said it was so romantic they were both at the same building and she dropped a box and he picked it up for her. Are you sure they met here and do you remember when that was?"

"I do. It was the day of the summer solstice. Archie was going fishing since he thought the fish might be biting better and I had a package—you see, I get my spices for baking via mail order from a special shop. Noelle always delivered them and this day she was getting out of the van and he had just parked his Jeep under the maple tree on the far side of the driveway. It's as clear to me today as it was then. When he laid eyes on her, Archie was dumbstruck. I'd say it was love at first sight. Noelle gave him a friendly but noncommittal smile. They exchanged pleasantries and that was it. She drove away and after the van left the driveway, he gathered his gear and went to the beach."

I crossed my arms over my chest, pursed my lips, and stared at the crackling fire. "Why lie? Unless he didn't recognize her the next time they met."

Minerva bobbed her head from side to side, contemplating this idea. "Possibly, but the way his face looked that first time, I don't think he'd ever forget her."

Tucking this tidbit away I would add it to my clue board when I got home. I asked, "Is there anything else you know about Noelle that might be helpful?"

Minerva's face softened as she nodded, her eyes filled with concern. "You're trying to determine if she could have struck out in anger and harmed him?"

"Yes." It was hard for me to believe that

anyone would hurt Archie, let alone the woman he was dating.

"Sadly, it is in all of us to some degree, to lash out at another. If she is your prime suspect, that will blind you to other information that must be brought to light."

That was a cryptic answer and once I had discovered she knew both my primary suspect and Archie, I thought it would be a concrete answer. "Are you saying she isn't guilty?"

"That I do not know for sure. But you must continue to look with open eyes and don't let your feelings cloud the view." She held up the teapot. "Can I warm your tea?"

That was a very kind way to change the subject and maybe I was too close to the emotions of the case. It was something to think about as I held out my cup. I marveled at the attention to detail of the room. "The inn is lovely. Have you lived here long?"

"All of my life. My family built this house in late 1692. We relocated here from Massachusetts."

I could feel my mouth drop open. "Really?"

She gave me a side-eye and an all-knowing look. "Yes. In the beginning there wasn't much here, just a few scattered farms further inland. We purchased this land and built our family home. At first, it was just that, but as the times went on and more people passed through this part of Maine, we opened it as an inn welcoming all travelers. As the years went by, we began to offer home remedies to people—tinctures mostly. But we needed to be cautious since the hysteria about witches didn't die quickly. There are a few people in town who will still look the other way when I walk down the street. But for the majority, the Robinson family is well respected."

"How many children do you have?" I figured since she was talking about family, the inn would continue to flourish for years to come.

"As I mentioned earlier, I have three nieces who are like my own daughters. But that is a story for another day if you can come back to visit."

"I'd love that." My tea cup was empty and I placed it on the tray in front of me. "Everything was lovely and I look forward to returning to the inn."

Minerva gave my hand a squeeze. "When my nieces arrive, you must come for lunch and meet them. Someday they'll be running this inn and it would be nice if they had friends close by."

"I would like that." Standing, I ran my fingers down Milo's back.

He did his long, lazy kitty stretch and looked at me. "It's time we get back to Pembroke Cove. You still have to stop at the post office."

I scooped him up and Minerva walked us to the door. Before I could leave she said, "Wait just one moment. I have a little something for you."

She left the room and came back with a long rolling pin tied with a deep red bow. "Please take this as a small token of our new friendship. You never know when it will be used."

I thanked her again for the gift and the information about the meet-cute for Archie and Noelle and we hurried to the car. Once inside, I buckled my seat belt and waited for the car to warm up a bit. "Did you know Minerva Robinson was a witch and might have some answers for us before we went in?"

He cocked his head and grumbled, "Lily, there isn't much about the magical community that I don't know. I hoped she could help and she did." He propped his paws on the dashboard and his head swiveled from the opposite side of the driveway to the direction of the beach that was hidden from view. "Do you think the first time Archie saw Noelle she didn't notice him, like more than a casual glance?"

"It's possible. If they saw each other in warm weather and he said they didn't meet until three weeks ago, something is off in the dating timelines. I'd like to talk with her again, but I don't believe it will provide us with any new information. Since she didn't mention it, he must not have made an impression on her." I eased down the gravel driveway and headed down Route One toward home. Destination: the post office.

The post office was quiet this late in the morning and I assumed it would get busy again around lunchtime. I approached the window and Etta was standing behind it, dabbing her eyes and sniffling. She glanced up and gave me a weak smile. "Hello, Lily. Can I help you with something? Stamps perhaps?"

"Hi, Etta. No, I don't need anything. I wanted to check on you. I can see you heard the news about Archie Dane."

She nodded. "It's all over town that he fell at the ice skating rink and hit his head. And what a shock. When he left work yesterday, he was so excited to bring his new girlfriend to town so that she could meet people. I got the impression he was pretty serious about her."

This was the opening I needed. "Had you met her yet?"

Fresh tears welled up in her eyes. "No, but I felt like I did. He talked about her constantly for the last few weeks."

So, the few weeks was the same line he had said to me. But I had no reason to doubt Minerva. "Had he mentioned when he first met Noelle?"

Dabbing her eyes with an already damp tissue, she thought for a moment. "I don't think he did. I'm sure he was out and about and noticed her. From what Archie told me, she's very pretty, a brunette with blue eyes."

Another wig and contacts. How did she explain that to him or did it even matter what she was doing? I was under the impression, at least for now, that changing wigs was like me changing shoes each day. "Etta, was Archie's route in town, the local businesses?"

"Yes, Chet Harvey has the route north and

a part of the western section of town, and for the south and remainder of the west side that would be Ellen Pease. There are just four of us who work out of this location full-time. We can get part-time help for the holidays if needed. However, with more people sending packages with other types of shipping companies, we're not as busy as we once were."

That was interesting. Archie had said he'd met Noelle when he was delivering a package and she had said it was at Robin's Café. At least that tracked since he would have been in town. "One last question, Etta. Do you know why a mailbag would have been found at the ice rink?"

Her face paled. "I was shocked when Dax brought it over earlier today. I had no idea something like that would ever happen around here. You hear on the news how mail and packages are dumped and never delivered, but I don't know why Archie would have done it."

I didn't point out that Chet or Ellen could have also dumped the mailbag at the event.

"What was in the bag? Just normal types of mail? Any important-looking packages?"

Etta looked around the empty post office and dropped her voice even though there was no one around to hear our conversation. "From the colors of the envelopes, I would say there were holiday cards, and a couple of very small packages for Bee Bee's Boutique, but nothing out of the ordinary for in-town mail. If I could scold Archie for being so careless, I would. Usually, he was a stickler for rules and he was an excellent employee." She made a *tsk-tsk* sound while shaking her head. "Has anyone let his girl know the sad news?"

"Yes, she was told last night." I wasn't going to let it slip that Noelle was asleep in his Jeep at the scene of the crime. That would surely be a juicy tidbit of gossip and one that didn't need to be spread around town.

The door opened and Alfred Schwartz from the Lights Out Theater strolled in. He said hello and moved to a row of mailboxes after we exchanged pleasantries. I thanked Etta for her time before I slipped out the door. So now I had two suspects, one Noelle and the other Chet. I didn't think Ellen would do something like this. Maybe Chet was the one who dropped the bag of mail and we were only assuming it was Archie, even if it did have mail for the businesses in town. Anything was possible in the game of cat and mouse.

Chapter 9
Gage

Walking into Robin's Café was always a mouthwatering-inducing experience. If I didn't know better, I'd say Regan was using magic to whip up amazing food that would entice people to come to the café. But she knew that was something that would go against the coven's rules, to ever influence anyone's free will.

Dax said, "Are we grabbing a table after we're done asking our questions?"

"I could eat and something sure smells good

too." I spied Regan at the back counter where she was talking to one of her waitstaff. Heading in that direction Dax trailed behind me as he nodded to a couple of customers. Regan gave us a friendly smile while she finished her conversation.

"Gentlemen, what brings you in today? If it's for the lunch special I have a turkey chowder and gobbler sandwich which is roast turkey, stuffing, and a cranberry mayo."

My stomach grumbled and I grinned. "That would hit the spot."

She looked at Dax. "And for you?"

"I'll have the same but before we sit down, can we talk?"

Regan blinked, taken aback at the directness of his approach. I gave him a sharp look and wished I could remind him to slow down. Taking the lead, I said, "I—we—do have a couple of questions if you have a minute."

"Am I in trouble?" Regan licked her lips nervously as she avoided Dax's penetrating gaze.

"Not at all. I'm sure you heard or saw what happened in the town square."

Exhaling, she nodded. "Yeah, I did. Very sad about Archie. Do you have any idea what he was doing at the rink so late?"

"Not yet, but Lily noticed the lights were on in the cocoa stand when she was driving home, which is why she stopped." I decided not to say anything about finding the mailbag yet.

She looked across the room and through the large windows in the direction of the skating rink. "I distinctly remember shutting them off. Gil Akers stopped over to hand in the coupons he hadn't used and asked if I'd leave them on. He thought the twinkle lights above the sign would look nice throughout the night."

"And you didn't?" Dax prodded.

"No. They would have looked nice but what was the point? No one would be at the rink so who would see them? I prefer to save the taxpayers' money and not leave the lights on. Besides there are the lampposts at either end of the square and then of course there's the lobster trap tree that's draped in twinkle lights. That was enough to highlight how pretty our town square is."

"Very practical of you." Dax drawled.

"Thank you." She flashed a relaxed smile at him. "Now that I think about it, wasn't it odd that Gil even asked? He's never taken much interest in anything to do with the Glow and Glide. But this year, he up and volunteers."

"I wouldn't think too much about that. Gil's always been a bit of a loner in town." I didn't need Regan to start talking about him to customers. One civilian making inquiries was enough. Lily and Nikki would be checking on the details. I didn't consider Nikki overly inquisitive but she was Lily's backup and extra witchy force. That made me smile, thinking of Nikki lifting her hand to provide support but so far, each time Lily had gotten into a tough spot, she had been alone. I shook off that disconcerting thought.

"Gage, are you feeling okay? Your face just drained of color, maybe your blood sugar dropped. Why don't you gentlemen grab a table and I'll bring your lunch over."

We walked in the direction of an open table where we'd have a view of the town square and people milling about. This way if anyone wandered too close to the ice rink, we'd be able to see who. With some luck, the guilty party would find his or her way back. Curiosity was often a powerful motivator in situations like this where the perp was unable to stay away.

I said, "We need to track down Gil Akers."

"What should I know about him?"

"A local, socially awkward. A classic loner but he took early retirement from the marina last year after he got a hip replacement. Also, we need to bump into Chet Harvey when he gets back to the post office. These guys might have seen something last night that will be useful."

Dax glanced at Regan. "She's right, are you feeling okay?"

"Yeah, I just thought of the tough spots

Lily's gotten into and it was like a knife through my heart."

"You know she's being extra careful."

"I do, but trouble seems to find her when she least expects it." I tapped the top of the table. "Back to the investigation."

He bobbed his head in Regan's direction. "You don't suspect her?"

"Nah. Feel free to chat her up, ask a few more questions, and maybe you'd want to ask for her number. Take her out on a date or even a spin around the ice."

His eyebrow quirked and his eyes widened. In a slow Southern drawl, he asked, "Did you forget I'm Louisiana-born and raised?" He pointed to his black Chukka boots. "These feet might be wearing boots suitable for winter weather, but they don't wear ice skates."

I couldn't help but smile. "Did Lily take you shopping again?"

He chuckled. "At least she's picking out more stylish options. Those first few plaid shirts weren't my style even though they're warm."

"You'll be glad you have them come January and she's practical." I had a few LL Bean shirts hanging in my closet. She had given them to me as birthday and Christmas gifts and I loved them. But it had more to do with the giver than the warmth of the shirt.

"Don't get me wrong, I appreciate all that she's done to help me get acclimated to the season."

"Hey, man, I get it. You're used to a certain look and it will take some more shopping to home in on your new style up here."

Regan was headed in our direction carrying an overfull tray. She placed bowls of steaming chowder in front of us. Next were the side plates that held thick sandwiches, a smaller plate with pickles, and finally two cups of hot coffee.

Dax took the napkins she held out. "This looks delicious. Thank you, ma'am."

"Enjoy." Her cheeks pinked and she bumped into a bistro chair as she went to greet some customers.

I nodded in her direction. "She'd say yes if you asked her out. Oh, and she's a witch too."

Dax dipped his spoon in the chowder and looked at me. "I'll think about it. Now can we circle back to the case?"

"Regan didn't mention the mailbag. Either she thought it was no big deal or it wasn't there when the stand was open." I took a bite of the sandwich and chewed while staring at her back. It was as if she felt me watching her and she came over.

"Gage, do you need something?"

Taking a different tactic, I went for the direct approach. "Why did Archie ask to store his mailbag at the cocoa stand last night?"

Her brow knitted in the center and she pulled out a chair and sat down. Dropping her voice, she said, "He didn't but that was strange and I should have mentioned it before. I pulled a wagon full of supplies from the cafe to behind the small hedge, you know the one that the stand butts up against?"

I put the sandwich down and she had my full attention. "I do."

"Well, I was running out of marshmallows and whipped cream, so I ducked behind the hedge for less than two minutes to get a bag and a couple of cans. When I came back, I nearly tripped over that bag. I have no idea who dumped it there. I shoved it under the shelf and forgot about it until you mentioned it. It was Archie's?"

"Why do you say dumped?" Dax was now paying close attention to the conversation. Not that he wasn't before but it would have appeared to Regan that he was.

"There was a small package and a few letters that had spilled out of the bag when I tripped. I shoved everything back in. Like I said, I stowed it under the shelf. I had customers beginning to line up and cold ice skaters mean they leave early if we don't keep them cocoa'ed up."

"Is that even a word?" he asked.

"I just made it up. Seems like it works, and

it's better than saying sugared up." A lightness had come back into her voice. She got to her feet. "If I think of anything else, I'll be sure to let you know."

After she left our table, I resumed eating and Dax did the same. "I shouldn't have assumed it was Archie's bag since it could have been Chet's or even Ellen Pease's. They were both there last night in addition to Archie."

"I think Chet was helping William. We should swing by The Sweet Spot and see if he noticed anything unusual last night."

"We'll go there next." I looked down the street. "I wonder if Lily's back yet."

"Hopefully she got more out of Noelle than I did."

I could feel Dax watching me as I ate. "Don't tell me not to worry. It won't do any good."

"Wouldn't think of it. I know if my fiancée was out tracking down clues to a murder, I'd be worried even if she was a witch."

I had to agree with Dax. Not all witches

followed the do no harm rule. Some strayed into the dark edges and that's when things could get very dangerous for Lily and Nikki too. "When we stop to talk with William, I'm going to pick up some cookies and coffee and drop by the bookstore. It gives me a reason to make sure Lily's back, I'll feel better knowing she's safe."

Dax nodded and gave me a knowing grin. "And if you're really lucky, she can fill you in on what she learned from Noelle and Etta."

"You know Etta?"

"We've crossed paths. She has her finger on the pulse of this town almost as good as Tucker."

That was another thread to tug. Running the hardware store for so many years, Tucker might have something to share regarding this situation. "I wonder if he has a machine to sharpen ice skates?"

"Do you think the skate that was found near our victim had been recently sharpened?"

"Hard to say. We can send it out to a lab to

confirm." Dax didn't mind that my answers were succinct. Why waste words when we were typically on the same page of how we approached investigating a crime. "Not that we'd get the results back fast. It would be more convenient if Tucker was able to tell us he did blade sharpening."

"Do most stores in small towns like Pembroke Cove have more than one hardware store, like in a town twice the size? It just seems like Tucker's Hardware is more of a general store from fifty years ago."

Dax's assessment was accurate and I couldn't help but smile. "It might be due to Tucker inheriting the store from his grandfather and I'm not sure how many other generations before that. It's a point of pride for him to have his roots firmly entrenched in our sandy soil."

We finished our lunch and I dropped several bills on the table, knowing we wouldn't see a check from Regan. I liked to pay for my meals and not accept special treatment. I pointed to the bills and gave her a wave as we made our way to the front door. As we wound our way through the tables Jill Dilly was perusing a menu with Katherine Reece-White, the owner of the local B & B.

I paused. "Hello, ladies. I highly recommend the turkey chowder today."

Jill unfolded a napkin and placed it on her lap. "Hello, Detectives. Another tragedy has struck our little haven again."

Just the opening that I needed. Jill and Katherine were part of the reliable grapevine network in town. This could possibly yield interesting results. "Yes. I'm sure you understand I can't confirm or deny anything specific."

Katherine leaned in our direction. "I heard that poor Archie didn't know how to skate. He was trying to impress his date after the rink closed down for the night. It's too bad he fell and hit his head, and that was the end of him."

Jill said, "If he'd been trying to impress that girl, she would have called for help when he conked his head. And don't you remember, he was headed to the state finals in skating when he was much younger. I'm guessing he could still skate."

Shaking her head, Katherine whispered, "Maybe he was there getting up the nerve to try some daring feat on skates and she was coming back later. You know how men are, always trying to do things they're not capable of doing." She shrugged her shoulders. "Sorry, Gage, but take my husband for example. He thinks he's a wiz at running the B & B, but the last time I left him in charge of checkouts, he didn't take final payments from three guests and there was no way I could charge them after they got a final bill marked paid from Donnie."

Jill said, "Maybe he should stick to booking treasure hunting adventures with people who come to town looking for that pirate treasure. You know it's supposedly buried somewhere around here from Captain Sam Bellamy."

The disdain in Jill's voice indicated how she felt about Donnie White's business, but this conversation was going in the wrong direction. However, it indicated one very important fact; these ladies didn't have any useful information on what had happened and it hadn't reached them yet that Archie didn't die from a simple fall on the ice.

"Ladies, enjoy your lunch," Dax said and I echoed the sentiment. When we got outside, I paused. "That, my friend, is how I tap into the very reliable network of the town."

"The average person does tend to know more than they think, but those ladies"—he looked through the window to where they were sitting—"are under the impression this was an accident. And we don't know any more than before."

I held up my hand and gave him a knowing grin. "But we do. If Archie was involved in something he shouldn't have been, it's still under the radar. This could be nothing more than a mistake—tempers flared and in the heat of the moment he was struck in the back of the head and fell to the ice. We won't know for sure until we get all the facts."

"Let me guess. Since there are no obvious suspects, the best way to get the facts in a case like this is to tap into all the locals."

I nodded in the direction of the hardware store and the bakery. "Onward to our next two stops and see what we can learn."

We were skirting the ice rink near the opposite end of where Archie had been discovered when my steps slowed. "What's that?" I pointed to a red object that stood out against the snow. I crouched down next to the bush and using a pen, I looped it through the red shoelace and slid it out. "Why, lookie here, the companion to the skate that was found at the scene of the crime."

"How do you know?" Dax snapped open an extra-large plastic bag that had magically appeared.

"If it's not the other skate, I'll turn in my badge. The red laces and pom-poms are identical and I don't think—" I snapped my fingers. "These aren't rental skates, but Noelle didn't know how to skate. Archie was holding her up. Who do these belong to?"

Being very careful not to rip the bag, we eased the skate in and zipped it up. As I scanned the area, I noticed Chet Harvey and Ellen Pease getting into their mail trucks and they were close enough to have witnessed what we found.

I nodded in their direction. "This news will get tongues wagging with the town busybodies long before we get back to the station."

Chapter 10
Lily

I was leaning on the counter as I filled Aunt Mimi in about meeting Minerva when Gage and Dax strolled into my store. Dax was carrying a cardboard tray with four to-go cups and Gage grinned and held up a white bakery box.

"Christmas cookies anyone? They're fresh from the oven."

I could feel the smile growing wider on my face as Aunt Mimi, with a tiny flick of her wrist, pulled up two chairs across from the wingback chairs in the small seating area. Milo slunk around the side of the counter and sat down.

He grumbled, "Do you think the big lug thought to pick something up for yours truly?"

Gage handed me the box, tipped his head to the side, and knelt down on the floor. Pulling a small baggie from his jacket pocket, he said, "And here's something just for you Milo."

My familiar leaned as far forward as he could without getting up. He sniffed the baggie and finally said, "Tell Detective Cutie thank you."

Dax smothered a grin and I gave him a look that hopefully put fear in his heart. If he ever breathed a word of my familiar's nickname for Gage, there would be no place in Pembroke Cove he could hide as I said, "Milo says thank you."

Gage rubbed Milo's head before opening the package and breaking the cooked cod into small kitty-sized bites, hand-feeding him. "I hope you like this kind of fish."

"He likes any fish that isn't swimming in an

ocean or lake." It warmed my heart to see Gage taking more of an interest in my cat. He always petted him, but going out of his way to get something just for Milo was sweet.

Aunt Mimi said, "We should enjoy our afternoon coffee break. It was a busy morning and I'm sure the afternoon will be just as hectic." She took a chair opposite from my usual one and Dax was next to her. It was funny how we always fell back into the same spots. I took the tray from Dax with the coffees and Aunt Mimi did the same with the box of cookies. We got comfortable and I selected a shortbread dipped in chocolate which I guessed would be flavored with a hint of orange. It was one of William's late wife Lulu's specialty cookies and something he only baked during the holidays.

I couldn't wait to hear about Gage's day of investigation and would happily share mine after. I didn't have much to tell other than how Noelle was high on my suspect list, but my only reason was that she was fake and both she and Archie had lied about when they met.

"How was the drive to Robin's Pointe?" Gage asked.

"Uneventful. I met with Noelle but before I tell you about my day, tell me about yours."

Dax snorted and Gage said, "I knew you'd want me to go first." He got up and went into the back room and returned with a smaller version of the clue board I had at home. "I'm going to jot down the notes."

This was a good sign. He was quickly coming around to share information with me. I crossed one leg over the other and leaned back in the comfy chair. "Who did you talk to today?"

"Regan, William, and Tucker. Oh, and Etta too." Milo hopped into Gage's vacant chair and proceeded to turn around three times and then settled in for a snooze.

Dax got up and adjusted the board so it wasn't facing the street but we could still see it clearly. "I'll be the scribe and you can fill the ladies in on all the details."

Gage picked up Milo and sat down. He

waited until Milo seemed to get comfortable in his lap before he said, "We stopped in to see Regan since I specifically wanted to know if she saw the mailbag. Apparently, it wasn't there when she arrived. Later in the evening she stepped behind the hedge to get supplies. When she stepped back behind the stand she tripped over the bag, and a small package and a few letters fell out. She stuffed everything back in the bag under the counter, she got busy and forgot about it."

Dax jotted down the highlights, and I said, "That makes sense. Cocoa is a big mover and cookies are second at this event. Why did you go see Tucker and William and most importantly, did you learn anything?"

"I was playing a hunch that we might luck out and they would have some dirt on Archie. This incident bugs me, like why kill this quiet mailman? It just doesn't fit."

I tapped my temple. "I've got something about that, but you finish first."

"Basically, neither Tucker nor William

knew anything, and William said his cookie stand was so busy he doesn't remember who was even at the rink last night."

I puckered my lips to the side of my mouth as if I had sucked on a slice of lemon. That was too bad; he was always a good observer. It was a shame he didn't recall anything. In his defense, his cookies would cause people to flock to his stand like seagulls at the beach. "And Etta?"

Gage gave me that knowing look. "You already talked to her."

Laughing, I said, "Of course I did. It's not like you'd tell me everything, even though the reverse is true." His eyes widened and I flashed him a sheepish grin. "Well, mostly."

Shaking his head, he said, "We don't have much to go on at this point. Other than we found the other skate near the rink today."

I leaned forward. "Go on."

"Do you know if rental skates come decked out with fancy laces and pom-poms?" Gage took a sugar cookie from the box broke off a corner and set it on his knee for Milo.

"They don't, but Noelle told me she borrowed them. I never thought to ask from whom. It didn't seem important at the time and maybe it's not."

Aunt Mimi was watching us banter back and forth before snapping her fingers. "I've seen those skates before."

I was surprised. "Why didn't you say something as soon as we started talking about them?"

She smiled and pointed to my forehead. "If you keep scowling like that, you'll get permanent wrinkles on your face."

"Aunt Mimi," I groaned. "Who owns the skates?"

"Ellen Pease has a pair just like those. I recall red is her favorite color; she says that it's festive."

"How would you know this?" Gage asked. "Not about her preference for colors, but that they're hers?"

"I don't know for sure, but if you look at the blades, she has an E on one and a P on the other. She's very fastidious about some things, which makes me curious why she would even lend them out, but you can find out the particulars when you talk to her, Lily."

Dax was writing the information down and Gage said, "We'll talk to her. I don't want Lily to become more involved with the investigation."

Quirking her brow, she focused her attention on Gage. "And do you think Ellen will tell you more than yes or no, that she is the rightful owner of them?"

"I'll have follow-up questions," he said.

"Maybe you and Lily could bump into her together and you can ask about the skates and Lily can ask any additional questions."

Dax nodded in agreement with Mimi. "That is an excellent suggestion and one that was staring us right in the face. Working with Lily will accomplish two things, Gage. One, you can play good cop and concerned neighbor which we know will play well, and two, Lily won't get into any situation that could be dangerous."

"See, Dax agrees this is a good idea." I wanted to slap him a high five, but I didn't want Gage to think we were ganging up on him. "What do you say?"

He tipped his head down and picked Milo up to face him. "What do you think? You're her familiar. Is this a good way to question Ellen?"

Milo squirmed in Gage's lap and glared at me. "Ms. Witch, does he think I'm staying home or at the store while you go off sleuthing?"

"Oh, Milo, you can come too if you want, but before we take off, we need to compare notes about our conversations with Etta. Then we'll go."

Grumbling that he'd stay and help Mimi, he hopped down and stalked from the seating area, disappearing around the corner in the direction of the children's section where he had a hidey-hole.

I scanned the clue board. "Who are the best suspects other than Noelle?" Rising from my chair, I began to pace the small area. "There's the unknown caller who we can call Mr. X who could be the attacker or a random assault is possible." Stopping mid-pace with my brain whirling, I said, "Did I tell you there is a discrepancy in Archie and Noelle's story about when they met? Which is odd since it wouldn't matter when they first met, but they both lied."

"No, you didn't. Spill the details. This could definitely be relevant." Gage grabbed another cookie and dunked it into his coffee.

"Archie told me that he and Noelle met a few weeks ago when they were both delivering a package to the same customer—she works at We DOT—but today I saw her behind a counter." I made a mental note to find out if she was a counterperson or just filling in for the day. "But when I had tea with Minerva Robinson, who owns the inn, she told me that Archie used to fish from her private beach. Anyway, last summer he met Noelle in the inn's parking area. He looked like Cupid's arrow had landed while Noelle was polite but uninterested."

"That Minerva doesn't miss a trick and is

excellent at reading people." My aunt must know about her special witchy powers of telepathy.

"Did they see each other again after that?" Gage asked.

"Not that she mentioned. But why lie about the first time they met?"

Dax was jotting down the information, adding the timeframe, and then glanced my way. "Maybe she didn't remember him. I never met Archie but after all that you've said, he was quiet and unassuming. It's possible it wasn't until the next time they met that something clicked."

"Or with all her changing of hair and eye color, could she be up to no good and it was only recently that he became useful?" I pointed to the board. "Write that down; it's a strong possibility."

"Lily, what's the motive for killing Archie?"

My shoulders slumped. "That's what I haven't figured out yet. Have you been to his apartment?"

"No. We were going to head over there next. I wonder if we'll find another mailbag."

"Dax, when you took the mailbag over to Etta to look at this morning, were you surprised she jumped to the conclusion it was Archie who had dropped it at the cocoa stand?"

Gage said, "I thought you were taking that to the station for processing?"

He shifted from one foot to the other. "I was but I wanted her to take a look at it before I put it into evidence. If there was something critical like medications for a resident in the bag, I didn't want it to get hung up."

Gage's expression eased. "And was there?"

"No. But I'm glad I did. I had her wear gloves and take a look through it, and she said it had to be Archie's bag since the mail was from his route."

I took the chalk from Dax and added Archie's name next to the mailbag comment. "We're right back to where we started. Is it possible we could be wrong about Archie not being a good person? Good people can do stupid or even bad things."

Gage asked, "Did Etta have any additional tidbits that could be useful?"

"She confirmed that Archie only started talking about Noelle a few weeks ago and she thinks this was a tragic accident. Which circles us back to him being a nice guy."

Dax said, "Good people can do bad things if cornered. Who knows, maybe Archie got in over his head and didn't know how to get out. Which is why when Mr. X called, he met him at the rink."

It felt like we were just going around in circles. Pressing my fingers to my tired eyes, I focused on the puzzle in front of us. "Here's what we're going to do. Dax and Gage, you'll go to Archie's apartment and I'll meet you there after I stop at the post office and bump into Ellen. I'll ask about the skates and see if she knows anything about how Archie and Noelle met. We'll meet Nikki and Steve, along with Sharon and Mac, if they can come, at my house for dinner."

I narrowed my eyes. "What are you hiding, Detective? There is no way you wouldn't have already had Sharon and Mac go over Archie's apartment with a fine-tooth comb."

His face morphed into that *I'm innocent* look. "We still need to go over there."

I knew he had a job to do and I understood it was not something he needed to tell me all the details, but if there was anything of interest in that apartment, he would have acted on it. "I'm still meeting you there. Will you wait for me?"

He stood up and pecked my cheek. "You can count on it."

"Alright, let's divide and conquer this case. For now, folks think it was an accident. We need to solve the case before people learn the truth and start worrying about the safety of our town square."

Dax and Gage grabbed another cookie and headed to the front door. He turned to me before leaving and said, "Please be careful when you talk to Ellen."

I gave him a wink. "Always and don't worry. I'll come back with some good intel."

Dax chuckled. "You're turning into a superspy."

I laughed. "Not a chance. Just call me the puzzle master."

Chapter 11
Lily

I glanced at my watch for the third time in the last fifteen minutes. I was not a patient person by nature and waiting for Ellen Pease to come out of the post office at the end of her shift was wearing on my last nerve. I was anxious to get to Archie's apartment to take a look around. Shifting my almost numb butt in the driver's seat, I had to wonder how long it took to close out a mail route for the day. Didn't they just hand in their keys, empty mailbags, and leave?

After my bum had officially lost all feeling,

the side door opened and Ellen came out, not looking right or left but headed straight to an older gray four-door sedan. I pushed open the door, my backside forgotten, and nearly sprinted across the street, calling her name.

At first, I don't think she heard me since she kept walking and I slowed my pace. Appearing eager was not the way to get the information I needed. "Ellen?"

Her steps slowed and she glanced around. Was she worried about being seen together? "Lily, what are you doing here?"

I'm sure it seemed odd for me to be lurking at the side entrance to the post office, but this was a serious matter and I had to have answers.

Taking the direct but gentle approach was my best option. "I was hoping I could ask you a couple of questions."

Her eyebrows knitted together. "How can I help you?"

The surprise was evident in her voice. "I wanted to talk about Archie." I didn't come right out and hit her that he was dead, going the tenderhearted route.

Her face crumpled and tears hovered on her lower lashes. "It's just awful." Her voice broke and even a heartless person would be saddened by the look on this poor woman's face. "And I heard you found him?" Shaking her head, a few tears slipped from her eyes. Using the back of her hand, she wiped them away. "I wish I could ask him what he was doing at the rink after it closed, and to fall and hit his head when he was alone with no one to help him is just..." She trailed off, at a loss for words.

I placed a comforting hand on her arm. "I'm so sorry for your loss. I had no idea you were so close."

A weak smile tugged at one corner of her mouth. "He was like a goofy younger brother and he was a good friend to my son Wyatt. Ever since his dad moved away, he's needed a positive male role model in his life and I was lucky Archie was willing to be that for him."

Now I really felt bad. Not only had she lost

a co-worker and friend, but her son did too. "If there is anything Gage or I can do, please don't hesitate to ask."

She nodded. "Thank you. But you didn't track me down to hear my tales of woe. How can I help?"

"It's easy to see that you and Archie were more than co-workers, so tell me, had you met Noelle before?"

"Before what?" Her eyes narrowed and her forehead was creased.

"I understand they met months ago and only recently started dating." It was the best way I could think to phrase the question that popped into my mind first. I had to know why their first meeting was a secret.

"The first time Archie laid eyes on that girl, he was a goner. I think it was last summer, but she wouldn't give him the time of day. He did his best to bump into her by going over to Robin's Pointe every couple of weeks to eat at Magical Moonshine—it's a pub—since he thought most people would eat there at least once during the week. I guess it's pretty popular."

"And did he finally see Noelle again?"

She nodded. "Yeah, two months ago maybe. He was so excited to see her and it took a couple of conversations before she gave him her phone number. And don't get the wrong idea, he wasn't stalking her or anything creepy. He just really wanted to meet her." Her face got all sad again. "Archie said he knew from that first time he said hello to her that she was the only girl for him."

"Sounds like it took a while for Noelle to come around. He needed some major patience with that girl."

"That's Archie; he had the patience of a saint. So when he asked if he could borrow a pair of skates to take her to the rink for the town event, I said sure. I wanted to be supportive and do all I could to help him like he's helped me."

"It's lucky you and Noelle were the same shoe size."

"Eight is pretty common." She glanced at

my size eight boots. "I have those too, nice and warm."

It made her point without any further conversation about footwear. "Do you know if Archie was upset or arguing with anyone?"

"Not that I know of. Why was something said? I won't have anyone besmirching his reputation." She folded her arms across her stomach and glared at me as if trying to get me to spill my guts that someone was speaking ill of the recently deceased.

"No, it's nothing like that. Noelle mentioned he got a phone call last night and was upset. Since you knew him well, I thought you might know why."

She didn't hesitate. "Everyone liked him and he never had a cross word to say about anyone either. They broke the mold when that man was made."

I agreed with her but I needed to know if it was really a case of his kindness being an act and underneath that exterior, he was really a first-class jerk. "Is there anything else that you can think of that I should know?"

"Lily, why are you asking all these questions? Do you think something bad happened to him? I mean, other than the obvious."

"You know me, Ellen, the local who loves to tie up all the loose ends of anything and everything."

"Here's all you need to know. Life wasn't fair to Archie and he deserved better than what happened. And if Noelle had been with him when the accident occurred, he'd still be here now."

"Like if she was with him when he went back to the rink?"

"Yeah. I saw them as they were leaving. That's when Noelle piped up and announced she was cold and ready for the date to be over. I could tell he was crushed."

I was shocked and if those were the words she'd used, Archie had to have been hurt. "Did she actually use those exact words?"

"Verbatim. I wanted to wring her neck and

that's when I knew she was not the girl for him." She withdrew her car keys from her pocket and said, "I need to get home. Wyatt's taking this pretty hard and I want to spend some time with him before dinner."

I took a step back from her car. "Sure. I understand, and remember, if you need someone to talk with your son, I know Gage would be happy to spend time with him."

"Thank you, Lily. That's really nice of you. I'll keep that in mind." She clicked the door locks on her car and got in.

I slowly walked across the street to my car. There were a few things that our conversation uncovered, but the most important point was Noelle didn't care about Archie so why did she agree to date him? Maybe something at his place would give me a clue into this short-lived relationship.

· · ·

I parked in front of Miss Judy's Dance Studio. It was fully decked out for the upcoming holiday. Two charming Christmas trees flanked the front door. They were decorated in pink and white lights, pink-and-white-striped bows, and tiny dance slippers. The wreath on the entrance to the studio echoed the pink-and-white theme. The door to the left of the main entrance led to the apartments upstairs.

I took a deep breath, steeling myself to climb the wooden stairs in front of me. I had gone into other houses of people who had passed, but there was something about this time that caused my feet to not want to move. I reminded myself the reason I was here—to help put the responsible person behind bars. With that thought uppermost in my mind, I climbed the stairs, each step cementing my determination to do what I must do to help Gage close this case.

When I reached the top there were three

doors. Miss Judy's apartment was easy to identify, it had a wreath identical to the one on the studio door. I wasn't sure which one was Archie's. I paused and marched over to door number two and gave it a sharp knock. The door swung open and Sharon was standing on the other side.

"Lily, come on in." She handed me a pair of latex gloves. "Just in case."

"Thanks. Are you coming over tonight?" I pulled off my winter gloves and stashed them in my pocket and replaced them with the latex version.

"I am, but Mac is going home. The baby has a terrible cold and is fussy so he wants to give his wife a break."

"I hope she's going to be okay."

Sharon closed the door. "I guess she's better than she was, but you know first-time parents and all; it's been tough on them." She pointed down the short hallway. "They're in the kitchen."

I walked in front of her as she said, "I heard

you stopped and talked with Ellen Pease. Want to give me the highlights? I'm going to her house next."

"Sure, but that might not be the best idea. Could you question her tomorrow? She's taking Archie's death really hard."

"Yeah, I can give her the night." She bent over and opened a cabinet door and began to look through the contents.

I entered the back half of the apartment which looked out over the harbor. The views were spectacular and I paused. Why would Judy not live in this apartment with the ocean view instead of looking out over the street? Not that it mattered, but from my perspective, this was amazing. Gage was looking through a stack of magazines on a side table, and Dax was thumbing through what appeared to be mail. There was a hand-crocheted afghan on a footstool in front of a leather chair, an empty coffee cup on the table next to it, and stacks of books on almost every surface. I had no idea he was an avid reader. I wondered why he rarely came into my bookstore. Not that it mattered now.

I tried to keep my tone light since this place looked as if Archie had just stepped out for a minute and he'd be back soon. "Hey, team."

Dax looked up and said, "How did it go?"

"Fine." I wasn't sure if Gage wanted me to share the details here or wait until we were gathered at my place. However, since Sharon was planning on talking with Ellen, I needed to fill in a few details. "Ellen and her son were pretty close with Archie and, in fact, he was spending time with Wyatt since his dad left town. Sharon said she could hold off talking with her until tomorrow. I wouldn't want to have undue stress added to an already difficult situation."

Gage nodded and his eyebrow cocked. "Sure, that won't be a problem. But you found out a few things?"

That gesture was telling; he was very intrigued since it was obvious Ellen and I had a good chat. "Yes." That was all I was willing to say just in case there was even a slim chance someone could overhear us. "What have you found here?"

Taking my cue, Gage said, "Not much. Typical guy apartment, frozen pizza in the freezer, cold cereal in the cabinets, stacks of clean laundry, and drawers are empty." He flashed me a grin. "Sort of like my place."

Dax piped up. "For the record, not mine. I like my clothes in drawers and cooking is my relaxation."

That got my attention. "You cook? How did we not know this? After tonight, you're cooking dinner for all of us."

"Then you'll be eating a Louisiana specialty."

Gage cleared his throat. "If you are done making dinner plans, can we focus on the job at hand?"

I felt sufficiently chastised and surprised. If I didn't know better, I'd think he was jealous of Dax and me bantering. Deciding to follow his lead, I wandered into the bedroom which was clean, just not overly tidy. I saw what Gage meant about piles of clothes on every surface. I picked up one stack at a time and set it down, working around the room. Looking for clues was less exciting with the police on the other side of the wall. Wait until I told Nikki we needed to venture out on our own and get our Sherlock on. Picking up the next to the last stack, a piece of paper fluttered to the floor. Bending down to retrieve it, I noticed a box under the bed. I grabbed the paper and then pulled the box out. Flipping open the top, I withdrew my phone and took a bunch of pictures before calling out, "Gage, guys, you need to see this."

Gage was first in the door followed by Dax, Sharon, then Mac.

"What did you find?" Sharon dropped down beside me and pulled the box close. "Whoa. There is a pocket-size notebook with dates, what looks like dimensions and another number. Some of them are in the low hundreds, some in the thousands."

She handed the notebook to Gage, and I stepped around her so I could get a better look. After all, I found it and lost it in the span of two minutes.

"What do you think this means?"

Gage glanced at the next few pages. "He wasn't collecting stamps."

Sharon held up another notebook. "This one has dates and the same sets of numbers."

I regretted not looking deeper into the box before I had alerted Gage. That book might have better information than the pictures I had. Was it possible I could get a few snaps before they went into an evidence bag?

"Anything else in there, Peabody?" Mac asked.

"Just a pen and a matchbook from the Magical Moonshine Pub."

"Who prints matchbooks anymore?" I held out my hand. "Can I see that?" She passed it to me and I opened it. Inside was a phone number. Could it be Noelle's? "This is where Archie met Noelle two months ago."

Gage held out his hand and I gave him the matches. "Somehow I don't think finding these matches and the notebooks is a coincidence."

I agreed. But the next part of the puzzle to solve was how did they fit. What information was he investigating, or could it be a logbook of items that he was tracking for personal gain? Too many questions and zero answers.

Chapter 12
Gage

I drove Lily in her car back to her place. We had swung by my house and picked up my rescue dog, Brutus. Now, the Great Dane had taken over the back seat. Dax would drive my detective's sedan and meet us at her place after a quick stop at the station where he would log the evidence Lily had found. I was sure there was nothing under that bed when I had gone into the room. Did she use magic to find it? I glanced her way and her head was tilted back against the seat, eyes closed, deep in thought.

"Potion for your thoughts?"

She opened her eyes and slowly looked my way. I lifted a shoulder. "It's one of my mom's favorite sayings so I thought I'd try it out on you."

"Potions. I will have to ask Aunt Mimi about those." She looked out the window. The darkness was creeping over the ocean toward the land. "She said Nate decided to bring the lobster boat in this year; he's going to make some upgrades."

The casual conversation was Lily's way of clearing her mind so she could tackle a puzzle from a different angle. It was something she had been doing for as long as I had known her. "Is he thinking about selling the business and enjoying his retirement?"

"I'm not sure. Nate's turned over running the boat half of each week to his first mate. Adam does a good job from what he said. Maybe he'll take over permanently at some point."

I clicked on the blinker and eased into her driveway. "And we're home."

Still lost in thought, she drifted into the house and went right to the pantry closet, and pulled out the clue board as she called to Milo. I closed the door and flicked on the overhead lights.

He trotted into the room and stretched out next to Brutus who had made himself at home on an oversized pet bed. Lily shrugged off her coat and gave me a cautious smile. "Now don't get mad but before I called you into Archie's bedroom, I took a few pictures of the notepad. I'm going to print them and have them ready to discuss after dinner."

"Lily." I threw up my hands. "You have to stop bending the law to suit your curiosity."

Popping her hands on her hips, she said, "Would you have shown them to me tonight?"

She had me on that one and we both knew it. "What am I making for dinner?"

"Spaghetti and meatballs. Nikki will bring

the bread and dessert, and I think Sharon is bringing a salad."

"When did you have time to arrange all of that?" I crossed the room and slipped my arms around her waist. "You're full of surprises."

She tipped her head to the side and looked at me. Her soft sable eyes and the smattering of freckles always caused my heart to flip in my chest.

"I am a witch you know, and I've got spells you haven't seen yet." Standing on her tiptoes, she brushed her lips on mine.

Now my heart went into hyperdrive. We were engaged but I was looking forward to when we got married. I could see us standing in this kitchen every night after a long day, doing this very same thing. A rap on the door interrupted the romantic moment.

The door opened. Nikki, Steve, and Dax strolled in. "Hey, you two," Nikki said. She glanced at the empty stovetop. "Would you like for me to lend a wand and get dinner started?"

Lily placed her hand over my heart and said, "Sure. We were talking about the case."

Dax cocked an eyebrow. "Is that what you're calling it now?"

I chuckled and gestured from Lily to me. "That's what we call it, but you and I have a totally different meaning when we say it."

He pretended to wipe beads of sweat from his brow. "Thank the stars." Rubbing his hands together, he said, "How about I make dinner since I keep showing up empty-handed."

Headlights flashed over the window. Peabody had arrived. "Dax, can you do it the non-magical way?"

He took a step back. "Are you implying I can only add value as a witch?" He chuckled and proceeded to crack a few knuckles. "Stand back and watch a master at work."

Nikki's laugh sounded like a cross between a groan and disbelief. She gave Dax a wink. "Don't worry, I can do a bit of magic on the sly before we eat if necessary."

He responded, "That won't be but if it

does, I'll do my own magic, thank you very much." He pulled open the fridge and peered inside. "Italian okay for everyone?"

Peabody took that moment to stride in, a bowl of what I guessed was salad in one hand and a bottle of wine in the other. She grinned as she scanned the room. "Did someone say Italian?"

Lily had taken the opportunity while chaos ensued during dinner prep to print the images she had taken at Archie's apartment. She was hanging them on the cabinets near the table and the clue board. Then she added the notes we had talked about at the bookstore onto this board. By the time dinner was ready, so was Lily. I set the table and played host. Milo and Brutus were starting to stir from their nap which meant they both needed dinner too. I had a container of dog's food in the pantry and I knew what to give Milo so I went ahead and prepped their dinners. I had been keeping an eye on Lily as she studied the pictures with the series of numbers from the notebook. The crease of lines between her eyes had been deepening which indicated the possible answer wasn't coming to her yet.

Dax turned from the stove with an oversized shallow bowl in his hands. "Dinner is ready." We all took our usual places at the table and Lily said, "Does anyone mind if we talk about the case while we eat? I really need to walk through this from the beginning and talking helps."

Peabody said, "Sounds good. It will help all of us to see things more clearly. This case is confusing. I know I can't get a handle on the motive."

As the food was passed around the table and everyone filled their plates with spaghetti with Bolognese sauce, salad, and homemade bread, Lily kept glancing at her board. I had never seen her this perplexed by a puzzle.

"Alright," she said. "Let's start with what we know, the basics. Archie started dating Noelle a few weeks ago and he wanted to bring her to Winter Glow and Glide. Since she'd never skated before, his good friend Ellen Pease offered to lend her skates. When Gage and I met Noelle, she seemed sweet and captivated by Archie, as he did with her. We left around eight and came home, driving one car. About eleven, we went back to my store to get my car. Gage headed toward his house, me to mine. That's when I saw the lights on at the rink. Archie was in the middle of the ice with a life-ending head wound, a single loaned skate nearby, and later that night, Noelle was discovered asleep in Archie's Jeep."

Dax said, "She claimed she grew sleepy with the heat on and drifted off. She had no idea Archie hadn't come back but from what she said, he got a phone call while they were driving back to Robin's Pointe and he said he needed to meet someone. And it would only take a couple of minutes."

"At which point why, after ten minutes, didn't she go looking for him? It was freezing out; there were icy spots on the sidewalk, and he could have fallen." Lily shook her head.

"There was the first hole in her alibi. The second, I discovered Noelle and Archie met months ago in the driveway at the Robin's Pointe Inn. And we also know from Ellen that Archie was going to a pub—Magical Moonshine—in hopes of meeting her."

I jumped in. "Which must have paid off since they began dating."

Tapping her fork on her plate she exclaimed, "Exactly. But why did they lie about it? It wouldn't have mattered to anyone when they met and started to date. Maybe Archie was embarrassed that she hadn't initially been interested, but why would she hide it too? This is a question that needs an answer."

I nodded in agreement. "Tomorrow I'll have a chat with her and see if I can find out."

"Good. Now let's talk about the mailbag behind the cocoa counter. Regan said it wasn't there when she opened but discovered it later. This leads me to think it was either left in hopes she'd find it and take it back to the post office or whoever left it planned on coming back for it after the event ended." She slapped her hand on the table and Milo's head snapped up, causing him to meow loudly.

She glanced at him. "I'm okay, little man." Rising from the table, she picked up the chalk and scrawled next to the word mailbag – *Coming back later* and then circled it.

"There is the major clue. Whoever left the bag was planning on coming back for it and when Archie arrived back at the rink, he interrupted whoever it was. A struggle for the bag took place and Archie fell, hitting his head. So, we can assume he never met the caller."

"Unless..." I hated to derail her train of thought. "What if the person who left the bag was the same person who threw the skate at him, and then he fell and hit his head, causing his fatal injury."

She underlined Noelle's name with the chalk and added the number one. "Which takes us back to her. The skates were in her possession, but why would she throw one at Archie unless she was trying to stop him from doing something and leave the other behind in the bushes."

"She was mad and threw it to get his attention?" Nikki asked.

During this conversation, Steve and Peabody had been pretty quiet. I asked, "Steve, since you haven't been involved with all of this, what do you think?"

"That Lily is right and Noelle did it. Nikki told me about the changing of hair and eye color thing and that she wasn't into Archie. In my experience, girls don't keep dating a guy they're not into. It's like one, maybe two dates and if there's no spark they move on. It wouldn't matter how into her Archie was; ultimately, the girl can put the brakes on things pretty quick."

Dax was nodding. "I didn't think of it that way until now but Steve's right. Lily said she wasn't all that upset that Archie died, not that it's the only reason but when we put it all together, we need to find the motive and arrest her."

Peabody said, "I'll run a background check on her first thing tomorrow."

"And Nikki and I will find a way to bump into Chet and Gil. They might have seen something at the rink. Maybe Chet has a theory about the mailbag."

This was a good collaborative effort on working through the puzzle and Lily had been instrumental in connecting the dots. "Lily, did Etta tell you that the mail was from Archie's route?"

She ripped a slice of bread in half and slathered it with butter. "She did and said she was shocked because Archie was a stickler for the rules and was an excellent employee. Oh, and one other interesting tidbit. Archie told her that he met Noelle while they were both delivering packages to Robin's Café."

"I've never seen We DOT vans in town. Do you think that's odd?" I asked no one in particular.

Steve placed his knife and fork on a now-empty plate. "I don't recall ever seeing them around. And wrecker calls take me all over the Cove and surrounding area."

I gave Peabody a nod. "Definitely check into Noelle Webber and dig up all that you can find even if she got detention in school. Something's not right."

"You got it, Detective."

"And if you come up dry, let me know and I'll reach out to my former colleagues. I'm sure they'd be willing to check into her background as well." Dax began to stack the empty dishes.

Lily gave him a wink. "And for the record, you should give Gage cooking lessons. Dinner was delicious."

In a slow drawl, he said, "Thank you, ma'am. I'd be happy to give your fiancé lessons."

I cleared my throat. "Let's get back to the case, shall we? We can focus on my cooking skills another time."

Flashing me a sweet and loving gaze, Lily continued. "Are we all in agreement Noelle is our primary suspect and for the sake of this conversation, they had an argument and in a fit of rage, she threw the skate, hit him on the back of the head, he fell, and she left him there?" She finally took a breath.

"That is plausible but how does the mailbag connect?" I didn't want us to lose sight of this clue; in my gut I knew the two events were connected. "Noelle wouldn't have access to the bag since it's not likely Archie wouldn't have had it in his Jeep."

Steve rapped his fingertips on the table. "There was a day last week when his mail truck was out of commission. It needed brakes and for that day, he used his vehicle to make his deliveries."

"Could a bag have been forgotten in there and when he discovered it, he stashed it behind the stand?" Lily asked as she shook her head. "No, if he had found it, he would have either left it locked in his Jeep or already have taken it back to the post office. Mr. X brought the bag, but how did he get it?" She pressed the palms of her hands over her eyes. "I'll ask Noelle tomorrow. If Archie had it in his possession, she would have seen it."

"Assuming she'll tell you the truth. Why don't you let me tug on that line of questioning with our primary suspect?" I wanted to point out that if Noelle had been angry enough to strike out at Archie, there's no telling what she might do to Lily if she felt backed into a corner. But it wouldn't sway Lily from talking with her.

"Fine. Nikki and I will talk with Gil and Chet."

She agreed far too easily which did nothing to alleviate the chill that raced down my spine.

Chapter 13
Lily

The next morning the sun was beginning to rise in the bright-blue sky and I woke refreshed. I needed to get to the bookstore by seven-thirty. Nikki was going to meet me there and our first task of the day was to be at Chet's mail truck by seven forty-five. We planned to ask him a few questions about the mailbag since by now Etta would have questioned him too.

I flicked back the covers, taking care not to disturb Milo who was still snuggled on his pillow on the side of the bed. I slid my feet into cozy slippers and hurried to the bathroom to get ready for the day.

By the time I got into the kitchen, the magic of the coffee pot had a rich, aromatic brew waiting for me. Milo was snoozing in the chair. "Good morning, sleepyhead." I poured a cup and took my first sip.

He grumbled something that sounded like good morning, but I wasn't one hundred percent sure.

"What's on your agenda for today?"

"Sleep." That was clear as a bell ringing. He opened one eye to barely a squint. "You?"

"I have several people to question in relation to Archie's untimely passing. Chet Harvey, Gil Akers, and I'm going to talk with Noelle too."

"Didn't Gage ask you to let him question her?" His eyes burst open and I could see the spark of interest. "Does that mean we're going back to Robin's Pointe and have time for tea with Minerva?"

"Yes to the first; yes to the second, and no to

the third. It's the holiday season and I can't expect Mimi to cover the bookstore every day. I thought I'd call We DOT shipping and ask about Noelle's route, that's if she really has one. My plan is to track her down and hope she might be more open to speaking candidly if I catch her off guard."

He slumped to the cushion as I burst his bubble about tea with Minerva. "I thought she was transparent yesterday."

That seemed like weeks ago and not simply twenty-four hours. "I don't trust much that came out of her mouth and remember she stuck to the story she just met Archie, not that they met months ago."

"Then I'm going to just hang out at the bookstore for the day." He closed his eyes again and grumbled, "Wake me when it's breakfast time."

I nudged the chair he was on. "Hold on there, spark-a-lina. I wanted to ask what you thought about the conversation last night with the gang."

He pushed himself to a sitting position and shook his little head at me. "To address your phrase, first, I don't like that new nickname. It sounds like you made it up and second, I've been dying for you to ask me about the case, and it only took you ten hours. But I have thoughts."

I knelt next to him, feeling bad that he felt slighted. Rubbing between his ears as they flattened in contentment, I said, "I'm sorry, Milo, but you know how I get when I'm trying to work through a puzzle. Never think your input isn't valued or wanted."

Without looking at me, he said, "You're forgiven, my dear witch, on one condition."

I laughed. He did love to bargain with me. "And what's that? An extra helping of smoked salmon as a treat? A bowl of kitty milk?"

"After the holidays, I'd like for us to go back to Minerva's again. There is much she can teach you over a cup of tea and I think it would be important for your education."

If Milo thought it was something I needed

to do, then we would. "I'll call her after the New Year and we'll make plans." He purred with contentment as I kissed the top of his head. I stood to fix our breakfast.

"Oh, and you need to get to Boston and obtain your own wand. It's time you get started with those lessons too."

"There's a wand store?" This was the first I had heard of it.

"Of course there is." He began to clean his face with his paw, effectively ending any further questions about wands.

Once I was sitting at the table and Milo had finished his bowl of fish delight from the chair, I broached the subject of the case. "Do you think I'm on the right track with Noelle being the one who hurt Archie?"

He began running his paw over his whiskers. "You have a thirty-three percent chance of being right. At this point, you're on target, but you're getting tunnel vision when it comes to Noelle. Not that I don't think it's odd how she changes her appearance constantly or her lack of feelings about what happened, but have you considered Ellen Pease or Chet Harvey?"

I was stunned. Knowing Milo paid attention was one thing, but he called me out on how I'd been solely focused on Noelle. But Ellen and Chet? They were neighbors and friends. I toyed with my coffee mug. "Why do you think I should look twice at Ellen? She and Archie were co-workers and friends."

"Last night you shared with the group that Archie was spending time with her son, like a big brother relationship. What if Ellen had taken a shine to Archie romantically and felt that time spent with Noelle would mean that he had less time to spend with the boy and Ellen. That is a possible motive."

I didn't want to admit that he was right. To think that Ellen might be responsible was difficult to wrap my head around. I got up and added her name under suspects and then did the same with Chet. Turning to Milo, I said,

"Talk to me about why you think he's a possible suspect too."

"Access to mailbags, super quiet, and he was at the rink that night. Yeah, you said he was helping but not where. Was he with Regan at the cocoa stand or maybe at the cookie stand, either way he was there."

"He was helping with cookies. But there's no motive." I sank in my chair, picked up my mug, and wrapping my hands around it, I inhaled the delicious aroma of coffee. Maybe that would clear my brain. Talking more to myself than out loud, I said, "Do mail carriers vie for routes? Could Chet have wanted Archie's since it was in town and he had to travel the back roads every day?"

I sipped my coffee. "What if Archie knew that Chet was after his route? Chet could have taken a mailbag from the post office to set Archie up as irresponsible and Archie discovered there were shenanigans at play. When Chet called him after the skating event and told him what he had done, Archie went down there to get the bag before it was lost."

"And they got into an argument, which got even more heated and Archie hit his head after Chet pushed him." Milo's kitty grumble was filled with sorrow as he said, "Poor Archie. Trying to do the right thing. There's one problem. What about the skate? How does that play into this scenario?"

I had another, better idea. "That's good but a second possibility is Archie met someone at the rink, reason unknown. Noelle got tired of waiting for Archie to come back and instead of falling asleep as she claimed, she went looking for him. Whoever he was talking to put her into a fit of anger. She picked up the skate and hurled it at him. That's how the skate sliced the back of his head and the pain caused him to fall back. At this point, she had already stalked back to the warmth of the Jeep to let him finish whatever it was he was doing." I knew I wore a smug look when Milo glanced at me.

"You really want Noelle to be the bad person in all this."

I got up and took my now empty coffee mug to the sink. Even though I was a witch doing simple things the non-magical way, it just felt right. "I don't want to contemplate that Ellen or Chet had something to do with Archie's death. They were co-workers and friends." I checked the clock on the wall. "I'm going to head to the store. Are you coming?"

He stretched before hopping to the floor with a soft thud, and padded across the kitchen to wind his body around my legs. "I know this is hard for you. But try to keep an open mind."

I picked him up and rubbed my chin on his soft head. "You might be gruff from time to time, but really you're just a softie."

He patted my cheek with his paw. "Don't start telling people that, especially your detective. I want to keep everyone on their toes where I'm concerned."

I laughed softly. "You're like a wild and dangerous jungle cat?" I tickled that soft spot under his chin that always made his ears flatten and he looked like Yoda from the *Star Wars* movie. I kissed the tip of his light pink nose. "Consider your secret safe."

At seven-thirty, I walked into the back room of my bookstore and flicked on the overhead lights. Milo trotted in behind me and the door closed. "Did you do that?"

With a flick of his tail, he said, "Who else would have?" and trotted out of the room, disappearing, more than likely, to his favorite spot in the front window where he would snooze and keep an eye on the town too.

I withdrew my book of *Practical Beginnings*, my book of spells which I hadn't opened in days, and once again was behind on reading. Each time I opened the book, it showed me a spell I could use in the near future for whatever I was involved in. That was one of the reasons I was avoiding it. I didn't want to divert my attention to anything new. With the holidays and Archie's situation, my cauldron was overflowing.

A slight tap on the door drew my attention away from the book and I looked through the side window. It was Nikki and in plenty of time to get to the post office. With a snap of my fingers, the door unlocked.

"Good morning." She grinned as she walked in. "I saw that. Great idea to use a snap instead of a flick of the wrist."

I could see her pride and approval of my growing skills. As an accomplished kitchen witch, Nikki could do spells that I couldn't and vice versa. I discovered this when she offered to help me learn a spell and the page in my book of magic was blank to her. It was odd how magic worked.

"Hi. Are you ready for a busy hour or two?"

"Of course. I'm ready to fulfill my role as Watson to your Sherlock." She withdrew her wand from her wool coat pocket. "And I'm prepared."

Nikki was the perfect Watson. She was more patient than I was, an excellent observer, and her most important quality, she would support my ideas completely and back me up as necessary. Seeing her wand made me think. "Milo mentioned the wand shop in Boston. Maybe after the New Year, we can go shopping?"

"We're going to Boston to shop for my wedding dress and your dress too. We can add on another stop at Wanderlings Wand Shop."

"That's the wand shop in Boston? The one Milo mentioned it."

She laughed. "Of course, silly. Where did you think we got them from? It's not like we're going to try and make them ourselves. Can you imagine?"

I wasn't sure how I should respond to that so I changed the subject to the present problem. "For our investigation, I want to get to the post office parking lot by seven forty-five so we can talk to Chet before he leaves on his route. Then I'm going to call We DOT and ask what Noelle's route is so we can corner her for a few more questions and then Gil Akers. I want to know what he saw two nights ago."

"All that and be back to open the shop at nine?" She gave a low whistle. "That's a lot of ground to cover in just over an hour."

I picked up a paper from the counter and handed it to her. "That's why this will be on the door."

"Be back by ten." She gave me a quizzical look as her eyes opened wider. "I have an idea. Does your book have a spell to enchant the sign? If you're not back by ten, the sign will change in fifteen-minute increments."

Now I was intrigued. "This is a real thing?"

"You're a witch, so these kinds of things are possible." She gave me a little shove in the direction of my book. "Go on. Put your hand on the cover and with a clear mind, ask for the spell and then open the book."

I did as she asked and I looked at her over my shoulder. "Are you sure this will work?"

She gave me an encouraging nod. "Go on, you can do it."

I placed both hands on the well-worn leather cover and closed my eyes. I concentrated on the sign on my door changing if the door wasn't unlocked and silently requested a spell. The cover on the book became pleasantly warm and tingled under my hands. I opened my eyes and waited another moment before turning to a page in the middle of the book. Written on creamy-white paper, in the same perfect script as on other spells I had learned, was *Time Extender*, and then a few lines. I read them out loud. "Give me the time I need to seek what needs to be seen. For this I wish so it shall be." I looked at Nikki. "Does that sound right?"

Taking a step forward, she nodded. "Yes, the second part should be interpreted that you are seeking the truth and that is what needs to be seen. Take your paper and tape it to the door and then repeat the words. It'll work like a charm." She grinned broadly this time. "Pun intended."

I picked up the paper and a roll of tape and strolled through the bookstore, with each step gaining confidence that I could do this. Milo popped his head up and watched me approach the door and tape the paper on it. Then I took a step back and focused my intention on the paper. In a clear, sure voice, I said, "Give me the time I need to seek the truth that needs to be seen. For this I wish so it shall be." I paused, should I say it again for good measure?

Milo beamed. "Well done, Ms. Witch. Did you get that from reading the book?"

I flashed him a wide smile. "Nope, Nikki suggested I ask the book to show me the spell and it worked."

He nodded his approval. "Very well done, Lily. You're beginning to see the real power of your gift. Use it wisely."

I gave him a wink. "Keep an eye on things and I'll be back by ten. I have clues to track down."

Chapter 14
Lily

Nikki and I hurried down the street, past the police station, to get to the post office. We had to intercept Chet before he left to begin his route.

"Do you know what you're going to ask him?" Nikki was keeping pace with my stride without even so much as a hitch in her breath while I created visible puffs, hitting the cold air at a rapid rate.

"Not really. I find it best to just wing it in most cases." We made a right-hand turn into the parking lot and there was Chet loading bags of mail into the white truck with the USPS logo on the side.

"Chet." I hollered while I gave a big friendly wave. "Can we talk to you for a moment?"

A flicker of annoyance danced over his face before it became blank. "Morning, ladies. If you need postage stamps, Etta can get those for you at eight when the doors open."

"Thanks, but I just wanted to ask you a couple of questions."

"Sorry, Lily, but I need to get going. A lot of packages to deliver this time of year and I don't like working overtime."

I put my hand out and hovered over his. It was enough of an indicator he needed to slow down for a minute. "It won't take long." I wasn't going to play the *don't you want to help us find Archie's attacker* card since it might be him.

His eyes darted to Nikki who stood firmly beside me. "Fine." The tone in his voice was anything but cordial which, of course, increased my suspicion he knew something I needed to know.

"You were helping out at Winter Glow and Glide on opening night."

He rolled his eyes. "Yes, you and the entire town saw me handing out cocoa coupons and helping with the cookie stand. What about it?"

Oh, that snark needed to get toned down. Frowning, I continued. "Did you see Archie Dane arguing with anyone at any time during the evening?"

"No. He was too wrapped up in that new girlfriend of his, you know the redhead."

"Noelle Webber. I met her that night and he was captivated by her. Did you see anyone upset or grumbling about him?"

"I told you I didn't see nothing that had anything to do with Archie. Running for William and Regan had kept me on my toes from the time I got there until I left."

"What time did you leave?" Nikki asked.

"Skating ended at nine"—he began to tap his boot on the blacktop—"and I left at nine thirtyish. I helped get the trash to the bins and I walked with Regan back to her shop. She had two wagons she'd hauled over with supplies. I was being a gentleman. There's no crime in that, right?"

I gave Chet a good look, taking in the slow blush of pink in his cheeks. I wondered if he was interested in Regan. They were both in their mid thirties and she was a very pretty woman. Maybe that's why he volunteered—to get to know her better.

"Of course not. It was very nice of you to help her. One last question. Why would Archie have a mailbag at the event?"

His eyes flickered with surprise. "You know about that?"

"I do. Can you hazard a guess why it would have been at the rink that night?"

"I already told Gage and that new guy, Archie must have had it in his vehicle. We've been pretty busy the last few weeks and he might have gotten careless."

That didn't sound like the Archie I knew or

the one Etta thought she knew as well. "Was that something he'd done before? Keep a bag of mail in his Jeep?"

"Who knows what he did. It's not something I've ever done. But to each their own, you know. How he did his job was his business." He pulled open the door of the truck. "I gotta go."

I took a step back and watched as he got in and gunned the engine, not that they had power like a souped-up hot rod, but Chet was trying to make a point that he was done with me and Nikki.

After he drove away, I looked at her. "What was your impression of that conversation?"

"He wasn't a fan of Archie's and he could be telling the truth about not seeing anything that was going on. The rink was packed."

I stuck my gloved hands in my coat pockets, wishing I had remembered hand warmers since we might be spending a bit more time outside today. "How about we get a coffee and I'll call We DOT and get the lowdown on Noelle's location."

"I like this change in plan."

It was a short walk to The Sweet Spot and as we approached, I pulled out my phone. "I'm just going to make a quick call."

I tapped in the numbers for the shipping office and put the phone on speaker so Nikki could hear the conversation too. A man answered the phone with a chipper *good morning*.

With my fingers crossed for the fib I was about to tell, in one long rush, I said, "Hello, I'm Lily Michaels from Pembroke Cove and I was wondering if you could tell me what route Noelle has today? I'm expecting a package and wanted to make sure I was at my shop. I have a little something for her, you know since her boyfriend passed."

"Hi, Ms. Michaels. I'm Kevin Weeks, manager of We DOT, and Noelle has the town of Pembroke Cove today. If you want I can track your shipment and give you an estimated time of arrival."

Since I didn't have a package, I needed to redirect this conversation and fast. I said,

"That's okay. I've already checked and it says between ten and two. Noelle does have the town today?"

"Yup, like I just said." Kevin was so darn chipper for so early in the day. Must either be all coffee'd up or just a happy morning person.

"Excellent." I changed my voice to come across as more sympathetic. "How's she doing? Since Archie's unfortunate accident."

"Who's Archie? And he had an accident? Poor guy."

"Her boyfriend, Archie Dane. They had been dating for a few weeks."

"Huh," Kevin said. "I didn't even know she was dating anyone new since the last guy, Harvey something or other."

Nikki's eyes grew wide and her mouth formed an O. Knowing exactly what she was thinking I said, "I might be mistaken. Please don't mention to her that I called about Archie. I wouldn't want to upset her or her boyfriend, Harvey."

"Not a problem and if for any reason your

package doesn't show up today, just let me know. After all, our slogan and company name is; *We deliver on time.*"

Nodding, Nikki tapped her temple as if she had just figured out the name of the business.

"Thank you, Kevin. I appreciate your excellent customer service. Have a good day and happy holidays."

"Happy holidays to you and thank you for calling We DOT Shipping, where delivering on time is more than our job, it's our passion. Goodbye."

I slipped the phone into my pocket and opened the door to William's bakery. The scent of yeast, cinnamon, and other spices teased my senses. "Good morning, William."

"Lily, Nikki, this is a pleasant surprise."

I leaned over the counter and kissed the older man's wrinkle-lined cheek. "We are in desperate need of coffee." I eyed the display case in front of me. "And maybe a sweet treat too."

His green eyes twinkled as he wiped his

hands on the front of his apron. "I made a batch of scones from a recipe I found in Lulu's secret file—caramelized pears with dark chocolate chunks." His eyes got a little misty when he mentioned his late wife Lulu. She had been a vibrant part of the community before she passed away and her scones had been worth every calorie.

"I don't remember a pear and chocolate scone." I looked at Nikki to see if she did, but she was shaking her head. "We'll take two."

He snapped open a white bakery bag and added two scones while I fixed two cups of coffee at the self-serve station. "William, the night of the Glow and Glide, did you happen to see anyone arguing with Archie Dane?"

He slipped two decorated sugar cookies into another bag and placed it next to our scones. "I wondered when you'd get around to asking me about that night."

Getting closer to the counter, I said, "You saw something?"

He tapped the keys. "That will be twelve dollars."

He was still giving me the family discount. I handed him fifteen and stuffed the change in the tip jar. "William, are you stalling?"

"Lily, I'm just letting the anticipation build. And yes, someone was arguing with Archie toward the end of the night. It must have been just about nine. I remember since I was packing up the few remaining cookies and stashing the empty boxes in my wagon." He paused for dramatic effect before saying, "It was Ellen Pease. I'm not sure what it was about, but she was some mad at him, stamping her feet and waving her hands. It went on for a couple of minutes before she stomped off. It was easy to see the way her face was all red and blotchy she was not happy with whatever had gone on between them."

"What did Archie do after that?"

"He stood at the edge of the rink looking like he had just lost his best friend. Then his date came up and I heard her say that she was ready to leave."

"This is very interesting. No one mentioned Ellen and Archie argued." My brain was spinning with this new information, and I was itching to get it down on my clue board. Since there was time between now and when Noelle would be in town, we could enjoy the scones and coffee and update the board with these new details from William and Chet.

"If you think of anything else, will you let me know?" I scooted around the counter and gave him a quick hug. "If anyone comes around asking questions other than Gage, don't mention what you saw."

He held tight for another couple of seconds before releasing me. "You know if Lulu and I had a daughter, I would have wanted her to be like you."

My heart constricted. "That is the sweetest thing but William, I consider you part of my family."

Handing me the two bags, he blinked away

the moisture that had begun to gather in his eyes. "Sorry, girls, the holidays can be pretty tough for this old bird."

"Oh, William." I hugged him again. "Always remember you have me, Gage, and my whole family. Come for brunch on Sunday, okay? It's going to be at Aunt Mimi's house."

"She already asked me."

"Good. Now we need to go but we'll talk soon."

When we reached the door, William called after us, "Girls, be extra careful asking questions. I got a bad feeling about this."

With a flutter of my fingers, we hurried across the town square, past the ice rink and the remnants of the yellow tape still dancing on the breeze. With a shudder, I pushed open the door to my shop and the warmth of the space wrapped us in welcome.

"Milo, we're back." He was still on the window seat, sound asleep.

I handed Nikki the bags and began to tug off my jacket and drop it on the small side chair so that it was close to the door the minute I saw the We DOT truck. "I'm getting the clue board if you want to set up coffee."

My cell phone pinged with an incoming text. It was from Gage.

Interesting update. Noelle Webber is not her real name. Unsure who she really is but be cautious if you see her today. XO G

I sent him a thumbs-up emoji since zero questions came to mind, at least at this moment. I pulled the easel from the corner of the storage area and carried it out front. With it positioned it so that people walking by on the sidewalk couldn't see it I scanned the notes. Nikki handed me my coffee and a scone before I sat down.

"I just heard from Gage and in an interesting twist, Noelle Webber isn't who she says she is. He's still digging but that confirms one of my suspicions."

Nikki took the top off her to-go cup and

sipped. "Which is?"

"She's hiding from someone and that's why she changes her looks. A constant change is a protective shell and this further cements in my mind that she is guilty of harming Archie. Now all I have to do is prove it."

Nikki broke her scone in half and took a bite. Her eyes closed and she groaned. "Are we sure William isn't a witch? These scones are perfect and I couldn't have made them any better."

I answered almost on autopilot. "Maybe Lulu enchanted the recipe like I did with the door sign." My real focus was on Noelle Webber or whoever she was.

"Oh, I hadn't thought of that and are you sure she was a witch?"

"Yup. That's how William figured out I was. Remember he was with Gage and I the night that sign fell on him and I had to get it off using a spell I had just learned. William had faith in me when I didn't."

She took another bite and said, "I'm going

back and buying more of these and ask him to make them for brunch on Sunday."

I was more focused on my clues than on a party that was still three days away. Smacking my fist into my hand, I said, "What are we missing about this case? I feel like there is something right in front of me and I just can't see it. Why didn't Ellen tell me she and Archie argued that night? She led me to believe they were best of friends."

"Even best friends can fight from time to time." Nikki withdrew a cookie that was shaped in a circle and decorated for Hanukkah, complete with blue frosting and a cookie cutout menorah with dots of yellow for glowing candles.

"Yes, but in light of what happened, don't you think Ellen should have mentioned they had a quarrel? It might have something to do with how or why he died." I circled Ellen's name on the board and added a question mark. "Noelle is first, then Gil, and finally, Ellen and I will be having another chat.

Chapter 15
Gage

I had sent Lily the text about Noelle or whoever she was. This was an added twist I hadn't anticipated, but I was glad Dax's connections were coming through for us. The more information we had on the mysterious Noelle, the better.

I could hear Dax's leather shoes connecting to the tile floor as he strode down the hall into my office. With zero pleasantries, he said, "Did you tell Lily that Noelle has no history and to stay away from her?"

I snorted and slapped my hand on the desk.

"You've met Lily; don't you think telling her to stay away will propel her right into Noelle's path to start asking a ton of questions? Ones that might get Lily into a peck of trouble."

He plunked down in a chair. "Until we know why she's using a fake name, it would be best."

Leaning forward with my forearms resting on the desk, I said, "What I suggested was she keep her distance until we learn more. That has a chance of working."

He steepled his fingertips together with his elbows on the arms of the chair. "That might work." But by the furrow lines between his eyes, I knew his doubts matched mine.

"When do you think we'll hear back from your contacts?"

Lifting his eyes to meet my gaze, he shrugged. "Anyone's guess. It depends on how many layers they have to sift through and why. It's a good thing I was able to get a partial print from that water bottle in her garbage."

"That was a stroke of genius on your part,

but what made you think it might come in handy? I wouldn't have guessed to do that." His mind worked like Lily's when it came to puzzles. I was good but nowhere near their level.

"Remember me telling you about the chaos of that apartment? There was one area that was very tidy and that was a picture of a farmhouse. It was alone on a shelf and it didn't have a speck of dust on it. Wherever that house was it seemed to be very important. There weren't any other photos in the room. As if she didn't have a life, no family, no friends. People who usually live that way either can't or won't have a connection to their past."

I thought of my house. There were family photos on the refrigerator, several in the living room, and a picture of Lily and me in my bedroom. Even in my office, I had a picture of Lily, Milo, and Brutus sitting on my desk. "Makes sense to come to that conclusion."

"What are your next steps?"

"The autopsy report is due this morning. Once we have that, we'll know if this was an accident. Was the fall Archie's demise or had the laceration inflicted by the skate proved to be fatal? And I'm headed back to see Etta. Something is niggling at my brain; the mailbag is a part of this. I just can't figure out how."

"Either way someone will be held responsible." Dax stood. "Call me when the report's in. I'm going to take a run over to We DOT and talk to the manager there, Kevin Weeks. He might have information on Noelle that will help narrow things down."

"Stay in touch and when I hear from the coroner, I'll text you." I watched Dax leave but didn't get up. Before I went to see Etta, I was going to stop by my parents' place. I wanted to know if there was some way I could communicate with Milo other than waiting for someone to translate what he said. After all, he knew what I was saying, but for me, it was like he was speaking Martian.

. . .

Walking into my childhood home was like stepping back in time. Everything was exactly the same as when I was growing up with the exception of my dad's gray hair and my mom didn't seem to age at all. Was that part of her being a witch, that she would stay ageless, and would that be me and Lily in twenty-five years? It didn't matter if I was graying as long as I was married to the witch I loved.

"Mom, Dad. I'm home!" I laughed. It was something Dad would say when he came home from work.

"In the living room," came my mom's reply.

The house was an older Victorian with ocean views but didn't sit directly on the coast. Growing up here had been heaven. Watching Nor'easters roll in, the stunning sunrises and the way the water glowed during sunset was magical. I smiled as I thought of that word again. As a non-magical person, I understood the splendor of nature and real magic.

Mom was sitting in a recliner facing the water and Dad was watching the weather. "Hi, son," he said as he pointed to the television. "We might have some nasty weather headed our way."

Giving him an affectionate smile, Mom said, "We will be fine, Burke. It's merely a report. The weathercaster is the only job you can be wrong one hundred percent of the time. You keep watching and we'll hold our breath for the next update."

"Glinda, do you know something you'd care to share with your husband and favorite son?"

"I don't know anything specific, just that all will be fine." She lifted her cheek for me to kiss. "And Gage is my only son and will always be one of my two favorite humans."

It was the same conversation they had most times I stopped by. "Parents, I don't have unlimited time to enjoy this family banter. I have an important question for Mom."

Dad began to get up. "Time for coffee, son?"

I placed a hand on his shoulder. "Rain check." I sat on the footstool next to Mom. "I need your help or advice."

She turned in her chair, solely focused on me. "I'll do what I can to help."

"It's about Milo."

Her hand flew to her throat and I detected a quiver in her voice as she asked, "Is he alright?"

"It's nothing like that." Mom took a deep breath and slowly released it. "It's just that when I'm with Lily, Nikki, and Dax, they can hear what Milo is saying and there are times when I know he's talking about me. I was wondering if there was a spell or potion that I could use so that I could communicate with him."

Patting my knee like she did when I was a boy, she gave me a smile that was filled with empathy. "Your father had the same problem when he learned about my special gift and he met Sylvester. But there is nothing I can do to help you. Familiars and witches can only communicate between themselves and non-magicals just can't. It's to protect everyone."

I could feel my shoulders sag. "There's nothing?"

Tilting up my chin, she cupped my cheek in that sweet motherly way she had done for as long as I could remember. "Talk to him through Lily, see if you can work out some kind of signal. You never know when it might come in handy."

I tipped my head to the side. "Like the way Timmy and Lassie communicated?"

Laughing softly, she said, "If you like that analogy, then yes."

I knew it wasn't one of my best, but tonight I'd talk to Lily and see if we could come up with something that would be useful. I got up from the stool, kissed her cheek, and gave Dad's shoulder a squeeze on my way out.

Mom called after me, "See you at the brunch."

· · ·

While driving to the post office, my cell dinged with a text. I pulled off Route One and withdrew my phone from my jacket. Just what I had been hoping for, the report from the coroner.

Cause of death: Blunt force trauma to the back of the head which increased the rate patient became hypothermic. Estimated time of death, 22:30. Let me know if you have questions. Eli

I looked out the windshield as I digested this information. We left Lily's house at eleven and Archie was already dead. I jotted off a quick text.

Thanks for the info. Is TOD consistent with injury happening around nine thirty?

I waited for a moment knowing Eli had his phone in hand, just in case I had a quick question like this. I got my answer in one word.

Yes!

The good news, if there was any, was he wasn't transported from somewhere else to the ice so the evidence we had was the best we were going to get. I let Dax know the situation and continued my drive to see Etta. On the way there, I'd swing by the station and get the photos of the mailbag contents. We had to be missing something.

Beatrice, from Bee Bee's Boutique, was at the post office when I arrived with the photos in hand. I stood a respectful distance as she talked with Etta, but Beatrice was visibly upset.

"Etta, when I called the vendor, they said they have confirmation the jewelry was in the shipping box and they confirmed it by the weight of the outgoing package on the receipt." She thrust a small brown box over the counter. "Would you weigh this, please?"

Etta had a sour look on her face as she took the plain brown box. She placed it on the scale. "One ounce."

Beatrice thrust a paper to her. "This is the proof of shipment and it states it was four ounces. It contained a necklace, bracelet, and earrings for a very good customer. With Christmas approaching, he doesn't have his custom-made jewelry for his wife."

"Did you have it insured?"

This side of Etta was not what I would have expected. Frustration was building on her face and in her voice.

"Of course it was insured. That's not the point. I think someone stole it between the designer and here."

"I have no control over what happened to the package between the time it left Chicago and arrived in Pembroke Cove. What do you want me to do?"

"For starters, I'd like you to be a little more understanding and then put a claim in for me."

With a saccharine sweet smile, Etta said,

"That I can do. I'll get started on it right after I speak with Detective Erikson. He's here on official business."

Beatrice looked at me and nodded. "Gage." She strode to the exit and pushed open the door. "I'll be back at lunch to pick up my copy of the complaint."

"Fine." Etta gave her a dismissive nod as the door closed. She shuddered. "One of the things I hate about this job is cranky customers, especially during the happiest time of the year."

Maybe I should point out that she could have been a tad nicer to Beatrice since the problem wasn't her fault. "Any idea what might have happened to her package?"

Etta leaned on the counter and dropped her voice. "Sending jewelry through the mail is a mite tricky. People see the return address and know what's inside. It passes through so many hands between there and here. Anyone could have sliced it open, removed the jewelry, and resealed it, and if they were really good, they could do it without the customer ever realizing it." She nodded in the direction Beatrice walked. "Like her. She just ripped open the package and probably never even noticed something was not right with the seal."

"That's a federal offense, isn't it—mail tampering?"

"If the perp gets caught, it sure is. But these thieves are trickier than your run-of-the-mill kind. They know how to do it and some even put costume jewelry in so that weights are similar for the recipient. But this one didn't bother. Just sealed it back up according to what Beatrice said so all she got was some Bubble Wrap. And these thieves figure the packages are insured since they're high-dollar items, so they don't care. This isn't the first person in town to file a claim; we've had several. I don't like to think this is a trend."

"If you can think of anything I can do to help, be sure to let me know."

She nodded in the direction of my hand. "Thanks, Detective. Now, do you have some pictures you'd like me to take a look at? And ask the questions you have before we get interrupted. It's a busy time of year, you know."

I wasn't sure how many times Etta needed to slip that into the conversation, but I placed two rows of three images in front of her. "Does anything here seem out of place?"

Picking up the first picture, she carefully looked over every square inch and then set it down and did the exact same thing five more times. When she was done, she stacked them and slid them back to me. "Care to take a look and tell me if you see anything?"

I had looked at the pictures countless times and nothing jumped out, but had Etta seen something that I missed? I studied the first three as she had done and was looking at the fourth when something caught my eye. "Etta, is this what I think it is?"

She handed me a magnifying glass and I took a closer look. I then looked at the next two images. My heart rate was ticking up. I looked at her and said, "How many other packages have been reported missing contents?"

One side of her mouth teased a smile. "How many little brown parcels do you see?"

"Five."

With a slight nod, she said, "Bingo."

I gathered up the pictures and thanked Etta for her help. "Please keep this confidential. I don't want neighbors accusing neighbors since this might have happened before the package even got to Pembroke Cove."

"Don't worry. But I do need to report it to my boss and the higher-ups. The government will need to get involved while you're solving Archie's case."

"Etta, could Archie have been the thief or he discovered the crime and was trying to get someone to stop or, confess?"

She tapped the middle of her chest. "I don't care what anyone says about him, Archie was an honest man. He would never have stolen so much as a book of matches. He was one of the good ones."

"Thanks for your help, Etta, and please give

whoever needs it my contact information." I handed her a business card.

"For what it's worth, Gage, I know you're one of the good ones too. You and Lily won't stop until whoever is responsible for the thefts and for Archie's death is arrested."

Humbled by her faith in me and Lily, I clasped the older woman's hand. "Thank you, Etta. I'll do my best."

Chapter 16
Lily

I stood in the window of the bookstore where I had an excellent view of both sides of the street. As soon as I saw the We DOT truck, I was out the door and Nikki was going to cover the store for me. My gut churned I wasn't good at confrontation, but I had questions, and by the stars, Noelle was going to answer them.

At ten-fifteen, the white delivery truck came around the corner of Doenut Drive and eased to a stop in front of Bee Bee's Boutique. I grabbed my coat and pulled it on as I hurried through the town square, hoping to intercept Noelle before she went inside. But if necessary, I'd wait until she came out.

The door on the truck rolled up with a groan and clunk. As I rounded the back, Noelle had stepped inside and was scanning shelves that were affixed to the truck walls. She unlocked and opened a wire door, pulling out several small packages. Jumping back with a start, she placed her hand on her chest. "Lily, you startled me."

"Hey, Noelle, I didn't mean to, but I was hoping you had a minute?"

"I'm kinda busy." She held up the packages like I hadn't watched her take them from the shelf. She closed and locked the wire door and jumped down from the back, pulling the door down in one fluid, well-practiced motion.

"This will only take a minute."

She started tapping her boot on the pavement. "Make it snappy. I don't want to get behind schedule."

"Why did you lie about when and how you met Archie?"

Her mouth gaped open. "What are you talking about? We met at a pub in town."

I gave her a side-eye look and noticed today she had short blond hair and hazel eyes. This was the third different look so far. How many wigs did the woman have? "The first time you met was at Robin's Pointe Inn last summer. There was a witness."

"Oh that. You know, Archie said the same thing, but I don't remember ever seeing him before a couple of months ago when he offered to buy me a drink one night at Magical Moonshine." She shrugged. "I guess that first meeting wasn't that memorable."

I couldn't argue with that, and I guess I needed to take her answer at face value. "Talk to me about the night Archie died. He was driving you home and what happened?"

She huffed out a breath. "I have to go through this again? I already told the cute detective. I got cold and tired from skating and I asked Archie to take me home. When we were driving, he got a call from some guy and we turned around and came back to the rink. He promised me he'd be a few minutes and he left the Jeep running so I wouldn't get cold. Wasn't that nice of him?"

I nodded that it was and waited for her to keep talking.

"Anyway, while I was sitting there, I discovered the skates were missing and I was pretty sure we left them under the bench. I figured Archie would bring them back when he came. That's when I got sleepy and rested my eyes for a couple of minutes. Until the door was jerked open and I almost fell out."

"What time did you leave the rink?" I filed away the tidbit about the missing skates since that would explain how one was used as a projectile at the back of Archie's head.

She tapped her finger on her chin, making it seem like this happened eons ago. "Before nine?"

Why did she phrase it as a question? How

was I supposed to know? I kept my rising frustration in check. "How long had you been driving before you turned around and was the rink closed by then?"

"Not long and yeah, when we drove by, it was dark."

I perked up. "There were no lights on at all?"

"Nope. Archie told me not to worry, that he knew that place like the back of his hand in the dark. And it was dark except for the lampposts and Christmas tree lights... I wouldn't have wanted to be fumbling around over there."

"And it didn't worry you when he didn't come back right away?"

"Why should it have? He's not a little kid." Then she wrinkled up her nose and seemed to shrink in front of me. "Oh. Yeah. Hindsight, that should have been an indication that something wasn't hunky-dory." Her eyes grew wide. "Do you think if I had been there, I could have saved him after he fell and hit his head?"

"Noelle, that's a question that can't be answered." Since I didn't know the results of the autopsy, I had no way to give her any other answer. "Before you fell asleep, you didn't see anyone or hear anything?"

"Nope. It was eerily quiet." She glanced at her watch. "I gotta go." She pushed past me and there was nothing else I could think to say. Watching her walk into Bee Bee's, I looked up and down the street and noticed Gil Akers was sitting on a park bench in the town square, watching me watch him. Round two was about to commence.

"Gil." I crossed the snowy ground between us, taking care not to slip on the ice as I grew closer to where he sat. His steel-gray hair was partially covered by a well-worn knit cap that matched his green jacket.

"Lily." He looked me over; his icy-blue eyes mirrored the frown on his mouth. "What was all that about?" He nodded in the direction of Noelle's delivery truck.

"Oh, you know. Just chatting." I sat down next to him. "It was really nice of you to help out at the Glow and Glide the other night." Easing into the conversation was the best option.

"Doing my part, nothing more, nothing less." His Maine accent was thick as he said part; it came out like "paar." "More townsfolk should take an interest in these events. It's for a worthy cause, you know."

I nodded, agreeing with him. "Did you happen to see anything out of the ordinary that night?"

He gave me a steady look. "You mean something to do with Archie Dane getting himself conked on the back of the head and dying?"

That was one way to put it, if in a rather unkind way, and it was interesting that Gil knew how Archie died.

"Nasty business going on that night. Tossing mail around like people didn't care to get theirs. You know Regan could have tripped and broken a wrist or worse if she hadn't been careful. But no, I didn't see anything."

I kept the smile to myself. Gil Akers knew a

lot about what had gone on, more than most people. "Did you see Archie argue with anyone?"

He crossed one leg over the other and then did the same with his arms. "Can't say that I did. Well, except when Chet wanted to take that girl for a spin around the ice."

"Noelle, Archie's date?"

"That's the one. The three of them were exchanging some harsh words. Not that I could hear what was being said, but you know, I could tell by their faces and hand gestures."

"If you couldn't hear what they were saying, how can you be sure Chet wanted to skate with Noelle?"

"Now that I heard plain as day. It was after when things got heated. I got busy again, you know, handing out coupons and helping Regan where I could." He pulled a pipe from his inner jacket pocket and held it before saying, "I don't smoke anymore, but I do like holding my old pipe. That Regan is a nice young girl and I was hoping Chet would ask her to take a spin on the ice but that didn't happen. Probably a good thing since a fella shouldn't be trying to take another's girl right out from under his nose."

"You're right. What time did you leave the rink?"

"Regan had her stand packed up a few minutes after nine and I helped her take leftovers back to the café. I must have gotten home by nine thirty and went straight to bed."

Something didn't add up. "Did anyone help you and Regan?"

"Nope, just the two of us. There wasn't anyone left at the rink to help. And the last thing I did was snap off the lights at her stand. I wanted to make sure she didn't slip on the ice."

"Very chivalrous."

Gil seemed to perk up under the compliment. "Manners never go out of style, Lily."

"That is a true statement. What happened to the mailbag?"

His brow furrowed. "You know, I can't say.

I know that Regan pushed it under the counter after she tripped, but I don't remember seeing it after that. Guess it was still there." He turned on the bench to face me and looked me square in the eye. "I know what you're doing and you need to be careful." He patted my hand. "I'd hate to see anything happen to you because of all of this. It's as plain to me as the nose on your face Archie had an accident. I don't need to know any more than what I do. Just be careful."

Right there I ruled Gil out as a serious suspect because I didn't feel one bit of worry as he warned me to be careful. It wasn't threatening or scary; the old man was just concerned for my safety. "Thanks, Gil. I'll be careful."

His voice got gruff as he said, "See that you do." Rising from the bench, he tapped the edge of his cap as if it were a hat with a brim and headed in the direction of Tucker's Hardware store. Probably going in to chat with the people who gathered for a quick catch-up on the town's goings-on. I sat on the bench for a few more minutes, going back over what Gil had said. I slapped the middle of my forehead. "Gil said he helped Regan and Chet said he did. So, who was lying?" The only way to know for sure was to ask the one person who had benefitted from the help. Regan.

I burst through the door of Robin's Café and looked around. Regan wasn't in the front which left two places, her office or the kitchen. I poked my head around the swinging door which was both the entrance and exit to the heartbeat of the café.

May, the primary wiz of this kitchen, was in front of the stove stirring a large pot and she looked up. In her soft-spoken voice which had a hint of the South, she asked, "What can I get for you, Lily?"

"I was hoping to find Regan."

She bobbed her head in the direction of a closed door. "She's in her office but go on in. She thought you'd be by."

That was curious; she was expecting me.

"Thanks, May, and whatever you've got in the pot smells amazing."

She gave me a smile. "Thank you, it's potato corn chowder. I can send you with a container if you'd like."

"Make it two, please. Nikki's at the store and it would be a perfect lunch on a cold day like today."

"It'll be waiting for ya. Go on now." She pointed to the door with her free hand.

I walked through the kitchen and tapped on the door.

"Come in."

Walking into the tidy space was calming to my frazzled nerves. It had been quite the morning and I wasn't sure who to believe. I plopped into the chair across from Regan's desk.

"You look worn out." She closed the book she had been looking at and focused her attention on me. "Would you like some tea or coffee?"

"Thanks, but no. I can't stay and May is

going to fix me up with chowder on my way out."

"You won't regret one spoonful of that creamy goodness. It's one of my best sellers." Leaning back in her chair, she said, "You didn't come here to talk about soup, so how can I help you?"

I liked that she got straight to the point. "It's about the night of the Glow and Glide." I didn't want to say again that it was the night Archie died.

"I wondered when you'd get around to stopping by. That was such a sad ending to the night." The sorrow-filled look on her face mirrored how I felt.

"You know me, I follow where the clues take me." I hoped that didn't sound glib, but it was the truth. It had taken two days to hear these conflicting stories. "I have talked with Chet, Gil, and Noelle Webber. And some of the stories are consistent, but there is one statement that contradicts itself."

"Let me guess, it revolves around me?"

Nodding, I said, "Who helped you pack up the stand at the end of the skating party?"

Without missing a beat, she said, "Gil Akers. He had been my right hand all night. In fact, he made sure I got into my car after we put the supplies in the café."

"What time was that?"

"I was pretty much packed and ready to load my wagon carts at nine since most people stopped ordering cocoa around eight-thirty. I stored the cups and napkins under the counter so all that was left to pack up were the thermos jugs, marshmallows, and whipped cream. It didn't take but a few minutes."

"Did anyone else offer to volunteer?" For some reason I wanted her to say yes, that Chet had at least made the effort to help.

"No. Just Gil." Her gaze was probing as she studied my face. "Care to tell me what's bothering you?"

Instinctively, I knew Regan was trustworthy and I could share what I knew with her.

"Chet said he helped you pack up and pulled a cart back to the café."

Regan let out a hoot and clapped her hands together. "That little liar. He was too busy mooning around the rink after Archie's date to get a cup of cocoa, much less offer to help me."

This was the second time someone said Chet was interested in Noelle. "Do you think Chet and Archie could have gotten into an argument over a girl and it got heated to the point where Chet would have harmed Archie?"

The laughter evaporated from her voice. "Are you saying Chet might be responsible for Archie's death?"

I let out the breath from my lungs and my shoulders sagged. "I'm not sure what I'm saying but things aren't falling into place." I got up and thanked her for her time. What I needed now was to get back to my clue board and write everything down I had learned. Maybe seeing it would help clarify my jumbled thoughts.

"Don't forget your soup," Regan called after me.

Crossing the kitchen, May met me at the swinging door with a paper bag. "Lunch for you and Nikki and it's on me."

"Thanks, May." I stuffed some dollar bills into the tip jar on my way out the door. I needed to hurry back to the bookstore before the chowder got cold.

Chapter 17
Lily

Lunch was a distant memory and with the influx of customers, I hadn't had more than a couple of minutes to think about the case until I finally sat down in a wingback chair. When I did I realized I needed to know exactly what time Archie had left this earth and Gage must have the report by now. I shot him a text asking him to give me a call. I was looking at the circle around Ellen's name when my phone rang.

I smiled as I said, "Hello, my handsome Detective."

"Why, hello yourself, my favorite witch." I could feel the blush rising in my cheeks and I glanced at Milo. That was one of the endearments he used with me and I didn't have the heart to tell Gage I was my familiar's favorite too.

"Thanks for calling me back so quickly. Did you find out what time Archie died and the exact cause?"

I could hear the hesitation and I knew behind that was reluctance to share the details. But I needed to know to help him solve the case. "Gage, please, tell me."

"Blunt force trauma to the head, followed by hypothermia, and best estimate time of death was ten thirty."

I stumbled back and dropped into the chair.

"Lily, I know what you're thinking and don't go there, please. There was nothing we could have done. The rink was closed and we were enjoying our time together."

He was right but it still hurt to know that just

a minor change in our plans might have made the difference in a life being lost or not. I told myself to refocus and the only thing we could do now was bring the responsible person to justice. "Did you learn anything else of interest today?"

"Nothing I can talk about on the phone. Are you closing on time?"

The bell above the front door jingled and with a wipe of my hand, I camouflaged the board, and then waved at my customer. "Barring a stampede of shoppers, yes. Then I wanted to grab a quick bite to eat at the Magical Moonshine Pub. Care to join me?"

"Lily..." I knew that tone all too well. It was similar to when Ricky Ricardo said to Lucy that she had some 'splaining' to do.

"You don't have to come if you're busy. But I need to get to the bottom of why Archie went there so often. I don't think we have an accurate representation of the facts."

"What time are we leaving?"

His tone was flat and I knew I had won this

minor skirmish. "Meet me at the bookstore at five on the dot."

I made a kissy sound into the phone and disconnected. It was time to stop being the female version of Sherlock and become a bookseller.

The remainder of the afternoon flew by. Milo trotted over to the desk and hopped up as I was tallying up the cash drawer.

"A good day for book sales."

I glanced up and lost count and had to start from the beginning. "Yes, but hold on while I finish." I banded up the cash in my deposit bag and locked the cash register the old-fashioned way with a key and then for good measure a quick spell. I was discovering we couldn't be too careful anymore with the crimes that had been happening around our sleepy little town.

"Don't look now but here comes Detective Cutie and his sidekick, Detective Sweet Tea."

"Who?" I looked to where Milo was staring and sure enough, Gage and Dax were at the door. I moved my hand from right to left and the lock was released. I whispered, "Milo, you're incorrigible." Gage's eyes widened and Dax nodded in approval as the door swung open.

"I thought you'd be happy; it's a term of endearment. After all, I've been thinking about this since Dax saved your life at Halloween."

"Shh. We'll talk about this later." I greeted them with a smile. "Hi. You're right on time." I placed the deposit bag in my tote.

Milo gave me the sad kitty look. "On time for what? Dinner, I hope."

I ruffled the fur on the top of his head. "Sorry, little man, but we're going over to the pub in Robin's Pointe. I have questions and someone there has answers. But Nikki is stopping over to feed you dinner and when I get home, I'll have a special treat for you." Yes, I was bargaining with my familiar and I hoped it would work. He could get snarky when he thought he was being excluded from exciting events.

He gave me a side eye and grumbled, "Like what?"

"Your choice." This would definitely put me back in his good graces.

He swished his tail from right to left and part of this was for the show of deciding, but also because he was never speedy when it came to deciding on a treat. "Before you say no, hear me out."

Dax chuckled. "That's never good, Lily."

Gage looked between me and Dax. "What am I missing? Did he decide on his treat?"

"Not yet." Dax had covered his mouth with his hand and his eyes were crinkled in the corners. Not surprisingly, he found this amusing.

Milo sat up straighter and announced. "Sushi."

I groaned. "Where am I going to get sushi takeout in the middle of December between here and Robin's Pointe?"

"Ask Detective Sweet Tea if he has any ideas."

Dax did a slight bow. "I'm honored you gave me a new moniker. Finally, I'm a part of the family." He smiled at me. "And I have a way to get your very handsome familiar sushi as his treat tonight."

I scooped Milo up and kissed the top of his head. "We'll meet you at home in a couple of hours, okay?"

"Sure. But can't you drop me off since you're driving your car home? Besides, it's cold out there."

"We'll leave right after Gage tells me what he's been holding back all afternoon."

Milo's head swiveled in his direction. "Better spill it. My witch is very talented at unearthing the truth."

Gage said, "Before I share my news, Milo, you and I need to find a way to communicate with each other. At some point, we'll be under the same roof when Lily and I get married. I want us to have our own relationship."

Milo put his paws on my chest and pushed back, and looking me in the eye, he said, "Gage is serious?"

Dax took a step forward. "Milo put yourself in his shoes. It's like we're talking a foreign language that he will never understand. Can't you figure out a way to talk to him?"

He huffed. "I'll think about it, but you know if I need to tell him information like a Christmas secret, I have ways."

I pulled him close. "Doing this for me would be like another early Christmas gift and it would make me very happy."

Milo dipped his head for me to kiss. "When you put it like that, I can't refuse. All I want is for you to be happy and a good witch."

"Gage, good news. Milo will figure something out. Now that it's settled, start talking. I want to know everything you do."

"Condensed version. Someone is opening up small packages sent via the mail before they're delivered to customers. I happened to be in the post office when Beatrice came in today and she was very upset. A custom jewelry set had been taken right from the package and resealed to look like it hadn't been tampered with and that's not all."

I wasn't thrilled when he paused for the dramatic effect. I waved my hand in the universal speed-it-up motion. "Go on."

"All the packages in the mailbag that was found at the cocoa stand had been tampered with and Etta said this wasn't the first time people have filed insurance claims." Before I could pepper him with questions, he said, "To be fair, this could have happened at any point from shipping to receiving, but this is a federal crime. First thing tomorrow morning, the feds will arrive and you know that means we'll be losing this part of the case."

"And what did you learn about Noelle?" I looked to Dax for that answer.

"Witness protection. I don't know for what exactly, but she came into the program about a year ago. I'm still waiting on more information but it's a start."

That would explain the constant costumes. Making sure she wasn't recognized by anyone. "That makes some kind of sense. When I talked with her today, she said the first time she met Archie he didn't make an impression on her. It was only after she had seen him several times at the pub that she agreed he could buy her a drink and the romance blossomed from there."

"Did she use the word romance? Because that wasn't the vibe she was sending off when I took her home." Dax glanced at Gage who nodded.

"Even the night at the rink she was sweet with him but not what I'd call *into* him."

Smacking my hand on the counter, I said, "Oh, and get a load of this tidbit. Gil mentioned Chet had been trying to skate with Noelle that night and he and Archie had words about him trying to bust up the date. Seems all of this mess swirls around her."

"Do you think these grown men were fighting over a woman? I'm not buying it. It begs the question what were they arguing over? No woman is worth destroying a friendship."

Dax and Gage exchanged a look and he said, "There are exceptions."

"Will the two of you focus on this case? Dax, are you coming with us to the Magical Moonshine tonight? If yes, let's get going so we have a front row seat to the locals showing up."

"I'm going ahead of you so we don't all walk in at the same time, and since I'm a witch and from out of town, I'm hoping to draw some attention where I can ask questions and get away with them."

Gage nodded. "And then you can follow up with whoever you want to talk to and I'll just be your bodyguard." He handed me a stack of papers. "Before we leave, take a look at these. Every package in these pictures was opened and delivered empty."

Dax pointed to the door. "I'm going to take off and meet you there."

I looked up from the prints. "Okay, and we don't know you or we do?"

He smirked. "I'm just a tall, dark, handsome stranger from the Deep South."

"You got that right, Detective Sweet Tea."

Gage looked between the two of us and he shrugged with a slight groan. "Milo."

I studied each picture, shifting from one to another and back again. I went behind the counter and opened up the drawer where I kept pens and scissors and found the magnifying glass. Peering closer, I jotted down the names that were listed on the five packages. When I was finished, I said, "Gil is missing two packages, Beatrice two, and William one."

He nodded. "Do you think that means Gil should be back on the suspect list?"

"Are you saying you think it's the empty packages that are really what's behind Archie's death?"

Nodding, he said, "I'd play the lottery and be prepared to cash in the winning ticket."

I gave a low whistle. That spoke volumes since Gage didn't buy lottery tickets. "Other than the missing packages, Gil was honest about helping Regan that night. He told me about the argument between Chet, Archie, and Noelle too."

"Gil told you his version but we, or I should say I, need to question Chet on this argument and Noelle too."

Shaking my head, I said, "What if Noelle and the other person were in on it together? She confessed to leaving the skates at the rink."

"When did she tell you that?"

"Today when I talked to her. Pretty much everything that you know I do too."

Gage placed his hands on my upper arms. "Lily, please don't talk to her again by yourself. We don't know anything about her other than she's in witness protection, which doesn't mean she's squeaky clean. Even criminals are pro- tected when they agree to testify against someone."

"I'll be careful." Standing on my tiptoes, I slipped my arms around his neck and brushed his lips with mine. "I do love that you worry about me, but I'm very careful and my magic is getting stronger every day. It's not like I'm helpless."

"I know but you're a relatively new witch and in a dangerous situation, your magic might not be as strong as it will be one, five, or ten years from now."

I tipped my head and grinned. "Do you really think I'll keep getting stronger? Like then I could be your right hand in all your investigations. We'll be the dynamic duo of Pembroke Cove."

He tried to smother a laugh but didn't quite succeed. "We have one dynamic duo which is more than enough for one small town—you and Nikki."

I kissed him again and whispered, "I'm glad you have finally recognized that I've got mad magical skills."

Milo twined around my legs and coughed. "If you two lovebirds don't get going, you'll miss the after-work crowd and I won't get my dinner."

Reluctantly, I slid my arms from their

resting spot on Gage. "Milo is encouraging us to hit the road. I'll get my keys and meet you at my house."

He swept me into his arms one more time and held me tight while saying, "I couldn't bear it if anything happened to you."

"You have nothing to worry about. I've promised not to go asking questions any place alone and you know I'd never break a promise to you."

He looked me deep in the eyes and a chill raced down my spine. I might not be looking for trouble, but could it find me? That was a sobering thought and one I wasn't about to dwell on.

Chapter 18
Gage

The Magical Moonlight Pub had been a bust. Dax and I went over the entire night again as we drank cocoa at Lily's house. Apart from people being very curious about Dax's move to Maine in the middle of winter, being that he was a Louisiana native, it was a non-event. We did have a good brick oven pizza, but Lily didn't think that was a decent consolation prize. When I dropped her off, she had been down in the dumps that we hadn't found the connection to the pub.

I wanted to make it up to her so I'd swing

by the bookstore early this morning to cheer her up. But first Brutus and I would take a quick walk along the beach.

With a sharp whistle, he came lumbering into the kitchen. "Hey, boy. Ready to go for a walk?"

His thick tail wagged from side to side and he bounced up and down on his front legs. "I'll take it that's a yes." Clipping on his leash, we walked outside in the crisp morning air. At least the sun was bright. I was hoping the walk would clear my head and send me in a new direction with the case.

We walked to the end of the street and took the sandy path to the shoreline where the tide was on its way in. With the jetty to my right, we went left. The wind was stiff off the water, but this was my favorite place to walk and it seemed Brutus had adjusted from living in the woods to now being almost seaside.

In my gut, I knew the mailbag had been stolen and Archie found out. Which led me to the five empty parcels. Noelle was connected to the theft but I didn't know how. The why, was financial gain. The packages had been shipped by mail, not We DOT. At the moment the biggest question I had was why she was in witness protection.

My head ached. No, that wasn't it. All I had was pure conjecture that Archie even knew the mailbag was at the rink and I couldn't confirm that Noelle wasn't asleep in the Jeep when he was attacked. With confirmation from Gil that Archie had argued with Chet and Noelle earlier in the night, could Chet have been the caller demanding to see Archie? But why was it to clear the air about Noelle?

Brutus was plodding along next to me and would look up from time to time as if sensing I was troubled. It seemed that I was in a race to solve this before Lily did if for no other reason than to keep her safe. She could easily stumble on a dangerous situation and not even realize it until it was too late like when she discovered Dean Hartley's killer in his greenhouse.

"When we get back to the house, I'm going

to see if Dax has heard anything from his contacts. Noelle Webber has to be the key."

He wagged his tail and I took it as a sign that he agreed with me. I rubbed the top of his head. "Ready to head back?" Brutus did a one-eighty in the sand and began to trot a little and I jogged to keep pace with him. Up ahead, there was a man walking in our direction. At first, I couldn't make out who, but as we got closer, I realized it was Gil Akers. He lifted a walking stick in greeting.

"Gage," he called out, "it's good to see you out here."

I extended my hand to shake his. "Brutus needed some exercise and there's nothing like fresh ocean air to clear the cobwebs away."

He paused and looked out over the endless waves. "It does that, gives a person time to think."

"Definitely." This was a perfect opportunity. "Gil, mind if I ask you a question or two?"

"Sure, Gage. How can I help?"

"I've discovered you had a couple of packages delivered recently that had been opened, the contents removed, and then resealed."

He nodded and kicked some sand with the toe of his sneaker. "That's right. Two to be exact."

"Can I ask what you ordered?"

He tipped his head to the side as if contemplating his answer. "I guess I can tell you. One was a gold pocket watch circa 1887 valued at around five thousand dollars. The other, a mint condition quarter and that value was around 10K."

"Wow. I had no idea quarters were so valuable."

With a snort, he said, "Are you kidding? That's nothing. There are some coins that fetch over a quarter of a million dollars."

I had no idea Gil was a collector but that begged the next question. "Why have such valuable items shipped via the mail?"

"Up until recently, I've never had an issue. The items have always been insured but shipping in a simple brown padded envelope is like flying under the radar and I've been doing it for years. These last two shipments have been the only ones to ever get pinched. Well, I had two others, but they were much smaller in value."

"And you didn't report it to the police. Why?"

"It's a federal crime, not local. I filed claims with Etta and some fed called and said they were checking into it since I wasn't the only person from town this has happened to. It still makes a fella mad as a hornet whose nest has been kicked."

"I'm sorry that happened to you. If you need anything, you know where to find me."

Gil grasped my hand as older people tended to do. "You're a good man, Gage. Glad we have someone like you on the force to protect the people in our little town." He pointed his walking stick down the beach. "Best get back to my walk. Doctor's order."

"Have a good day." I watched as he made his way down the beach. I was going to make it a point to stop into Bee's and check on the value of her items too.

I tapped the side of my leg. "Come on, Brutus. We need to get back."

I went straight to the station after Dax had sent me a text that we needed to talk. Coffee with Lily would have to wait. He was waiting for me when I arrived. There was a coffee in the middle of my desk and a grim look firmly affixed to his face. I had seen that look before in the mirror and this was not going to be good news.

"Good morning." He pushed the coffee in my direction. "You might want to drink some before I tell you about my call from an old friend at my former office."

I took off the top and took a long drink despite how hot the coffee was. It was strong and preparation might be the key. "Go ahead. I'm listening."

"Noelle Webber is Nancy Chase. She's in

witness protection for testifying in a case for theft of jewels, rare coins, and stamps."

"I'll be a monkey's uncle." I put the cup aside and leveled my gaze on Dax. "In an ironic twist, I ran into Gil Akers this morning on the beach. He was one of the victims of the mail theft and stolen from him was a rare coin and an antique pocket watch. And he said this wasn't the first time either."

Dax interlaced his fingers and tipped his head back. "Noelle, also known as Nancy, with her access to a shipping company and valuable pieces like that, well, it looks like Lily was right and it has been Noelle this entire time."

"All that's left is to turn over this information to the feds and question her on what role Archie played in all of this."

He gave me a thoughtful look. "I've been thinking about the angle. My guess is she finally realized he could be useful in her scheme. Dating him could have given her access to information about his route and probably even while he was working so she could lift the packages. Somehow, she had to get the packages and by bumping into him while he was delivering and taking advantage of his infatuation with her, some guys can get distracted by a beautiful woman and let their judgment lapse."

"Want to ride along as I take a run over to We DOT? This needs to be done in person. With a little bit of luck, we can bring her in for questioning and by the time your old friends arrive, we'll have the answers we need."

He stood. "Give me five minutes. I want to make a couple of calls."

"Sure." I withdrew my phone from my shirt pocket. "I'm going to touch base with Lily so that she knows the case is all but closed and she can get back to focusing on her bookstore."

"Tell her you'll stop by with lunch and fill her in. This way she can relax."

In the short time period Dax had been around, he knew both Lily and me. Not only could she relax but I would as well, knowing she was working at what she did best, sell books. There might be a little part of her that was disappointed she hadn't solved Archie's case but she had played an integral role in the investigation. After all that we had learned about Noelle, or should I say, Nancy, this case had been full of twists. "I'll meet you out front."

He pulled the door closed after him and the gesture of privacy was appreciated. I called her cell and when she didn't answer, I left a voicemail. "Hi, sweetheart. Good news. We're bringing Noelle in for questioning and I'm confident by the end of the day not only will we have arrested the person responsible for mail theft but also for Archie's death. Love you and I'll swing by at lunchtime and fill you in."

By the time we got to We DOT Shipping, I was prepared for Noelle to come peacefully, resist, or even run. "Make sure you thank your buddy for coming through with this information."

Dax was looking out the windshield, his face grim. "It's helpful when all the pieces fall into place. In addition to arresting the responsible person for Archie's death, we've also helped wrap up a federal case. Not a bad day and it's not even lunch yet." He glanced my way. "Did you make plans with Lily for lunch?"

"I left her a voicemail and said I'd be over around noon. I'm sure the store was busy when I called or she was getting ready for a busy day." I parked in front of the nondescript building with the sign out front. "Let's go."

We strode into the small office and a man behind the counter looked up with a smile on his face that quickly faded. "I'm Kevin, the manager. How can I help you since it doesn't seem you're here to ship a package?" He looked from me to Dax and back again.

"I'm Detective Erikson, and this is Detective Peters. We're from the Pembroke Cove Police Department and we're looking for Noelle Webber. Is she here?"

He visibly gulped and nodded. "She's loading her truck out back." He pointed to the door behind him. "Can I ask what it's about?"

I moved to the door and said, "Sir, for your safety, please stay in here."

Dax said, "Do you know if Ms. Webber has a gun?"

The color on Kevin's face drained and he shook his head. "No idea."

I cautiously opened the door and saw Noelle. Her back was to us and she was loading boxes into the truck. Thin white wires trailed down from her ears and her head bobbed to the music I assumed was playing. Nodding to Dax, we moved quickly across the cement floor. When we reached her, she looked up and stumbled back, landing on her backside on the floor of the truck.

"Hey! What's the big idea? Scaring me half to death." Her gaze landed on Dax and she grinned. "Care to help me up?" She held out her hand and Dax clasped it, pulling her to her feet, but he didn't let go.

"Nancy Chase, you're under arrest on suspicion of mail fraud and for the murder of Archie Dane." I took great pleasure in saying those words. "You need to come with us back to Pembroke Cove where federal investigators are waiting for you as well."

She tried to wrench her arm away from Dax, but he held firm as he snapped on one handcuff, twirled her to face the truck, and snapped on the other. Once her hands were secured behind her back, she faced me.

"I may be a lot of things but I ain't never killed so much as a spider and even if I found Archie boring as all get out, I wouldn't have killed him. I didn't do it."

I wasn't going to debate with her in this warehouse. "We can talk about it when we get back to the station." Before she could say anything else, Dax recited the Miranda rights to her.

Stamping her foot, she yelled, "I'm telling you I didn't kill Archie."

We escorted her through the front lobby and Kevin called after us as we went outside, "Are you bringing Noelle back to work?"

We kept walking and I said, "Not today."

"Who's going to deliver all those packages? We have a reputation for delivering on time; didn't you read the sign?"

The door closed before he could say anything else. Noelle grinned. "On the upside, I don't have to go back there and work anymore. It was a snoozefest."

I got to the Cozy Nook Bookstore a little before twelve and there was a sign on the door that read, *I had to step out, but I'll be back at noon.* That gave me time to zip down to Robin's Café and pick up chowder and some rolls. I wished I had stopped at The Sweet Spot to get some cookies, but maybe Regan would have something sweet that Lily would enjoy.

Whistling Christmas carols, I strolled down the street, my steps light and thoughts carefree. Noelle was sitting in a cell and would be chatting with federal agents within the hour and Lily would be tickled to hear all the details.

When I got back to the store the sign now

read, *I had to step out, but I'll be back in fifteen minutes*. Well, that was odd but it gave me time to run across the square and get a box of cookies. I glanced over my shoulder at the shop, wondering what could be keeping Lily.

Crossing back across the square I could see the sign was still on the door. I set the bag and box on the ground and cupping my hands around my eyes, I leaned against the glass to peer inside. The overhead lights were on, but Lily wasn't to be seen. I rapped on the window and waited but she didn't come out of the back room. My heart rate ticked up and I grabbed my phone, hitting the speed dial button, hoping she'd pick up, but it went to voicemail. I left a hasty message asking her to call right away before disconnecting. I banged on the glass harder this time, causing my knuckles to turn red. Calling her name, I waited a few seconds before racing down the alley to the back door. I turned the knob. It was locked and I didn't have a key. I pounded on the wood with my fist, calling, "Lily!"

I felt the kitty door ram my shin and I looked at Milo. He began to meow and after all these years, I knew this particular tone wasn't just a chatty, give me some salmon, meow. "Milo, you have to give me a clue as to where Lily is. I know something is wrong."

He began to pace in front of the door and glanced at me, meowing the entire time. "I'm going to get Dax over here so he can open the store."

Before I could turn, Milo swiped my leg with his paw, his razor-sharp claws sliced through my pant leg, connecting with my skin. "Ouch, what the... Milo." But he wouldn't let go.

I pulled him off my pant leg and held him away from me so I could look him in the eye. "Look, I don't speak familiar so either figure out a way to help me, or I'm getting Dax."

He stared at me intently and when I tried to look away, he batted at my cheek as if forcing me not to break eye contact. I kept hearing the word home in my head.

"Milo, do you think Lily is at her house?" But again, the word that kept running through my brain was home.

I took off at a dead run with Milo cradled against my chest and pulling my phone out in the other hand. I was rounding the corner of Doenut Drive when Dax answered. Before he could say a word, I blurted out, "Something's wrong. I think Lily is at her place and I'm on my way there now. Meet me as fast as you can."

Chapter 19
Lily

I raced home to get my book, *Practical Beginnings*. I needed to get back to the store quickly but if there was any downtime I was going to read and practice any new spells the book might want to show me. Although Milo hadn't been reminding me about reading the book, which he had done on a regular basis since I discovered he could talk, I missed learning new spells. I wasn't about to try to magically get the book to The Cozy Nook. If something went wrong, not only could my family's book of magic be lost but it could fall into the wrong hands. Not that anyone who wasn't a Michaels could read it, but I wanted to err on the side of caution.

I passed Gil Akers on my way home and gave him a toot and a wave and the same to Chet delivering mail. Soon Noelle would be locked up and life could get back to normal in our little town just in time to enjoy the holiday season.

Parking my cute Mini Cooper, I left my shoulder bag and cell phone in the car since I'd only be a minute. Gage would be at the store in less than thirty minutes so we could have lunch and he promised to fill me in on some new developments.

Using my new spell to unlock the back door, I eased it open with a forward motion. Dang, I was getting the hang of this and Milo would be very proud of me. I could hear him now. *My dear witch, keep practicing and soon you'll be able to do all sorts of spells to make your everyday life easier.* Laughing to myself, I swung the door shut. There was no sense in heating the outside.

I hurried to my bedroom and paused to hang up a couple of shirts on the drying rack and then continued to where I was reading the book last. It was lying on the nightstand right where I left it. I pulled it to my chest, always feeling as if it were more like an old friend than a very old book.

I heard a faint knocking on the kitchen door. "Who on earth?" Avoiding the use of magic to just open the door, I hurried into the kitchen and peeked around the curtains. Gil Akers standing on the porch, clutching the middle of his chest.

I flung open the door. "Gil, are you okay?"

He looked at me, his knuckles white as he held his sweater in his fist. "I'm not feeling very well. Can I come in and get warm? I think I walked too far in this cold."

I took his arm and guided him into the kitchen. "Of course. Sit down at the table. How about a nice cup of my mom's tea? That will put the pink back in your cheeks."

"That's kind of you, Lily. I'm sure that would do the trick." He sat down and dropped his hand to his lap after smoothing out the front of his sweater.

"Are you having chest pains, Gil?"

"No, just a little out of breath. Maybe it's asthma or the doc said I might have a slight issue with pleurisy. Breathing in that cold air, I'm supposed to wear a scarf, but that's for people without my constitution. The tea will help, I'm sure."

I had to keep my smile in check when he started talking about his constitution. Who used that word in conversation anymore in conjunction with health? Placing the teapot on the counter, I selected a mint variety from my mother's blends. It was good to calm a cough and for breathing issues. I added the honey pot to a tray with two mugs and spoons.

"I bumped into Gage earlier at the beach. He was asking me some questions about mail tampering, mine to be specific. Which gives me hope he's close to arresting someone for killing Archie Dane."

Keeping my expression neutral, I asked, "Did he tell you the cases were related?"

"Nah, he didn't need to. With his mailbag at the scene of the crime and those packages being opened, it's easy to see he was up to some funny business. Don't get me wrong, I'm sorry he died, but committing a crime like that is just plain wrong."

"And Gage told you Archie was guilty?" This made no sense. We had never seriously discussed Archie being the person responsible. It had only been logical that he was trying to right the wrong. Everyone who met him would never have thought he'd be guilty of a crime.

"Well..." He dragged out that one word and it had me wondering what the conversation had really been. I wished Gage and I had chatted before Gil had ended up in my kitchen.

"Not in so many words but I knew what he meant."

The kettle whistled and he gestured to the pot. "Tea's ready."

I noticed the sleeve on his jacket was torn and I remembered seeing that color of fabric on the stand at the rink. Was it Gil who had ripped his coat at the scene of the crime? I poured the hot water over the tea infuser and the fragrance of mint wafted up.

"Who do you think called Archie that night to come back to the rink?"

I felt a finger of fear slide down my spine. That bit of information had never been made public so how did Gil know about the call? "What phone call?"

"Oh, Gage didn't tell you that someone called Archie when he was driving Noelle back to Robin's Pointe? Said he needed to get back to the rink. The girl left her skates."

Those were two tidbits of information that nobody knew about except the person who called. I turned with the tray in my hand and forced a smile to my face. Since Gil was being all chatty, I might be able to wrangle a confession out of him. How could I record it without him becoming suspicious?

Setting the tray in the middle of the table, I said, "Here we are. Would you like a few shortbread cookies that I made? Nikki's been teaching me some simple baking skills and they turned out quite tasty."

He narrowed his eyes. "I've heard you're not much of a cook. Do you remember that cake you donated to the town picnic?"

Gil brought up the only time I had baked in the last ten years for any type of public event and he was right; the center wasn't cooked. "Not to worry, these little cookies came out perfect. She even showed me her secret for rolling them to the perfect thickness for baking."

"I do enjoy a good shortbread cookie." He nodded, "Thank you, that would hit the spot."

I withdrew the cookie tin from the cupboard put a few on a plate and sat down with him. This conversation would be delicate to extract the confession so that he wouldn't realize what he had said.

"You never said; did Gage tell you about the call?" He took a cookie and broke it in half, dipping one side in the cup of tea he poured himself.

"He might have mentioned it but I'm pretty sure Archie wasn't responsible for the theft."

His brow shot up. "Why, what gives you that idea? I'll bet he and that girlfriend of his were in on it together since she'd know how to fence things."

"Noelle is a delivery driver." What the heck was he talking about? She was the one who in a fit of rage threw the skate at him and left him to die.

With a snort, Gil finished the cookie and brushed off his hands over the table. "You are either playing dumb or your boyfriend is holding back information or"—his eyes flicked with a wicked gleam—"you're really not as smart as everyone says. Since you've become this crime-solving legend around town, I figured you'd have the case solved, which is why

I've been strolling by your house for the last two days, hoping to bump into you."

I picked up my mug and sipped my tea as my brain raced for the different scenarios that could unfold. I certainly could call to Gage with a spell but the best way to help him was with a full confession. "You could have come into the bookstore anytime if you wanted to talk."

He shook his head. "Lily. I do like you, but this is a conversation is best between just the two of us. I need to extract a promise from you about my"—he tipped his head from one side to the other—"little involvement in the events in question."

"Why don't you tell me what's on your mind and we can talk about the next steps together."

Clucking his tongue, he again shook his head. "I can see you're looking for more information to pull all the pieces together and once you know everything, this will be your last teatime with me. I wanted to make it memorable, well at least for me."

That was certainly more ominous than I'd like but I had been in tough spots recently and if I had to, I could out-magic him since he wasn't a witch. "I'm not sure why you think this will be the last time we enjoy tea together." I sipped again and began to feel a tad nauseous. Pressing my hand over my belly, he leaned forward, watching me with interest.

"Lily, are you feeling okay?"

I was beginning to see two of Gil and wasn't sure which one I needed to focus on. "I'm sorry but I seem to be a bit wonky."

Both of the Gils in front of me gave me a sympathetic smile. "I'm sorry about that, but I need to know what you know before I leave town."

"Leave?" I closed my eyes and waited for him to answer. It seemed to calm my queasy stomach or maybe it was just wishful thinking on my part. Goosebumps raced down my arms.

Did he give me something that was going to kill me?

"I can hardly stay although I do regret leaving my home. I finally got it perfect, but I've packed all my collectibles and shipped them to my new location." He tapped his fingernail on the wooden table which sounded more like a jackhammer in my head. "And for the record, I did not use the United States Postal Service or We DOT Shipping."

"Am I going to die from whatever you slipped in my tea?"

"No, but I was told by a reliable source that you won't remember this conversation later to share it with your fiancé. Don't worry. It won't cause you permanent damage other than a minor memory lapse."

"What are you talking about? You drugged me?" As I struggled to maintain focus, I wondered how Gil had gotten his hands on a potion like this. Heck, I didn't even know they existed.

"Nope. I potioned you." He actually giggled and I cringed. "Do you like my new word? It seems to work in this context."

"Just lovely."

"You're mumbling a bit, Lily, please do try and speak clearly as I need a bit of information before I go."

I pushed my tea mug away and Gil pushed it back. "Have another sip." He pushed it even closer. "I must insist."

With a fuzzy brain there was no way I could come up with a spell to make the tea disappear, but I could cause a diversion. "After you tell me what you did and why." Even if he was right and I wouldn't remember, I had to know the why behind Archie's senseless death.

Both of the Gils in front of me shrugged. "Nutshell version, I have had several items stolen from my mail, valuable items, and Archie was my mailman. At first, I didn't think it would have been him, but after discovering he was going to that pub to see Noelle, who really is a thief, it all came together. When I happened to discover the mailbag in Chet's truck, I figured he was going to turn Archie into Etta but he needed to own up to what he did. I had to get the coin and watch back. I figured he'd tell me who he sold them to and it would be over soon."

"If Chet had the bag, why didn't you think it was him? Wouldn't that have been logical? You said yourself there was something going on between him and Noelle. They would make better partners. But was it you who called Archie to come back to the rink?"

"Well, of course it was. I told him I had the mailbag and if he wanted to protect his girl-friend, he'd better hightail it back there. When he arrived, Chet showed up so I waited in the shadows. I was about to discover what I needed to know—who the guilty person was."

I had to stay focused while Gil talked. My vision was starting to clear, but I wasn't about to let him know. I fluttered my eyelids as if I was trying to stay awake while I slurred the questions. "What was Chet doing?"

"I put an unsigned note on his windshield

telling him people knew about his girlfriend. You see Chet Harvey and Noelle had been dating quite a while. Once I arranged for Chet and Archie to meet at the rink, all I needed to do was wait. I hung out in the tree line waiting to get the scrap of fabric from my coat which had stuck to the cocoa stand before anyone discovered it." He rubbed his hands together. "And you didn't at first, which reminds me you should have worked on your observation skills more."

He leaned forward and with a malicious grin said, "Now, back to the Chet and Archie story. Each man thought the other had summoned him there and since they both were denying it, things got heated fast. Chet did admit to dating Noelle."

"She was two-timing on Archie?" I made sure my words had a slight slur. Then it clicked, he had said she was a redhead and not a brunette. The Glow and Glide was not the first time they'd met.

"Yeah, but they started arguing about the

girl and I needed the truth. Ellen's skates were under a bench so I crept over, keeping to the shadows. No one ever pays attention to the old man. I threw one, hoping to have it land on the ice and get them back to the important part of the conversation."

"But instead, it hit Archie in the back of the head."

"Yeah, it did. He stumbled and begged Chet for answers. It was like the blow to the head didn't faze him. I think the sight of blood bothered Chet though and confirmed he and Noelle had been working together to divert the contents in certain packages. Since Archie's mail route had mostly good parcels and he was infatuated with Noelle he was an easy target. Chet pointed to the mailbag I had left near the cocoa stand and once Archie saw it, he lunged for it. Sadly, he was unsteady on his feet and collapsed. Chet took off in one direction and before I could check on Archie, Noelle showed up. She looked around, then put the mailbag back behind the counter and took off, leaving Archie toes up on the ice."

"No one thought to look around for who threw the skate?"

"Crazy right? I guess they were so caught up in their argument it didn't register. By the time Chet left and then Noelle I think Archie was out cold."

I clenched my hands into fists. "You left too. Archie was unconscious and bleeding on ice and you didn't bother to call anyone?"

"I left the lights on, figuring someone would eventually check it out. And you did."

My temper flared at his smug response. "That's just great, someone did. Me. But I was too late."

He grabbed my hands and forcefully pushed the mug into them. "Drink or I'll pour it down your throat."

All my pushing for the truth had given me time to clear my thoughts. As I did with a door lock, I imagined the teapot in his lap with the hot tea as a distraction giving me time to escape.

He yelled in anger as the hot tea made its mark. I leapt up and ran to the door, wrenching it open. Gil was in hot pursuit, pretty spry for an old man with a hip replacement. With a glance over my shoulder, I saw he was brandishing a maple rolling pin.

Chapter 20
Lily

What was I doing, running down my driveway with a seventy-year-old non-magical man in hot pursuit threatening me with a rolling pin? I might not be a kitchen witch, but I knew how to use one of those. I stopped running and whirled around. Gil was gaining on me, but I needed to get him to drop the rolling pin. Too bad whatever he had slipped in my tea was still clouding my thinking. But with each step he took closing the distance between us, my thoughts miraculously cleared. I held up both arms as if I were about to conduct an orchestra. In a clear, calm voice, I said, "Rolling pins are made for baking, not bashing. I demand that Gil stop, drop, and roll it to me. Only then will he be set free. This I wish so it shall be." With a flick of both wrists, his feet seemed to freeze to the ground. It wasn't the most creative of spells, but it seemed to have done the trick. At least he wasn't gaining on me any longer. That was a small consolation.

He began to flail his arms. "Lily, you have to help me!" Panic was rising in his voice as he continued to keep a tight grip on the rolling pin.

"Once you drop your weapon, I will." I took a couple of steps in his direction and briefly concentrated on Gage, willing him to come to me. Milo's little face popped into my mind as if he was reassuring me he was on his way home. That was a little odd since he had never done that before or maybe it was wishful thinking on my part. Having that little fur baby was a balm to my soul on my toughest days.

Gil persisted in clutching the wooden

cylinder. "Lily, please come closer and as soon as you can unfreeze my feet, we'll sit down and talk this over. I've changed my mind. I don't want to hurt you, but I am going to demand my money back from that woman who said three drops of the potion would make you unable to stay awake, much less walk and talk or cast a spell."

"Where you're going, Gil, I don't think getting a refund of a few dollars will matter." I crossed my arms over my chest as I could sense Gage and Milo were growing closer. "Are you ready to give me that rolling pin before you hurt yourself?"

He clutched it to his chest. "How do I know you won't hurt me?"

I wasn't about to share with him that as a witch, I vowed to do no harm. It seemed what little he thought he knew about the witches of Pembroke Cove is they would do anything for a bit of cash, at least the one he met. It was easier to respond with one word. "Trust."

His face went purple. "Like I put my trust

in the post office and they allowed people to steal from me? I filed a complaint after the first time, but did anyone do anything? No. So trust is not something I do."

"Fine. Gage will be here in a few minutes, and he can disarm you once you're arrested for the murder of Archie Dane. But while we're waiting I have a few follow-up questions."

"Don't bother to ask. Maybe you should chat up Chet and Noelle since they're in this scheme up to their eyeballs."

I gave him a curt nod. "You know that's the smartest thing you've said all day."

A dark sedan came to a screaming halt in my driveway and another right behind it. The drivers' doors flew open and Gage reached me first, Milo and Dax were two steps behind him.

"Backup has arrived." Milo leaped into my arms and butted his soft head to my chin. Gage held us both in his arms while Dax wrenched the rolling pin from Gil's hands and glanced my way.

"Lily, is it safe to assume Gil Akers is under arrest for the—?"

He waited so I could fill in the blank. "For the death of Archie Dane and the attempted poisoning of me, which to be crystal clear, Gil, I am pressing charges."

Dax cleared his throat and held a proud grin in check. "Would you mind releasing him so I can transport him to the station for booking?"

I gave him a wink and snapped my fingers. Gil hurled himself forward in a poor attempt to make a break for it.

Gage grabbed him by the back of his jacket. "Not so fast." He escorted Gil to the back of Dax's car, he gave me a searching look.

"Call Mimi and have her give you something to eradicate the effects of the potion Gil slipped you. Lingering effects stink." He tugged my chin but before he went to his car, he said softly, "You're one witch I never want to cross. I can't imagine how strong you'll be a year from now. Well done, Lily."

I stood a little taller with the compliment hanging in the air. Gage came back and pulled me into a one-armed hug and kissed my temple. "Want to tell me what happened?"

"I will but we need to find Chet and Noelle; they're responsible for the stolen contents of the packages."

"Good news, Noelle's been arrested and is waiting in our jail. I'll have Peabody and Mac track down Chet on his route and bring him in too." His eyes softened. "Did Gil really try and poison you?"

I gulped when he put it that way and coupled with the fear in his eyes, it really brought home how close I had come. "On a bright note, and one I get credit for, I did not go poking around. This time trouble knocked on my door with a fake heart attack."

He shook his head. "True and that is never a good thing. But we'll figure out what to do about that later. Right now, I need to get your mug of tea as evidence."

"And I'm cleaning my kitchen too. I kind of

caused a pot of tea to spill into Gil's lap. I just hope the pot didn't break."

He snorted. "You have a brush with death again and all you can be worried about is your teapot?"

I gave him a sharp look. "It was a gift from your mother when I bought my house. That is priceless."

"Maybe she'll give us another one for a wedding present." He held me close as we walked into the house.

L ater that afternoon, I was sitting in the lobby of the police station, waiting for Sharon and Mac to bring Chet in. I wanted to be on hand to get his version of the story. Noelle was already chirping like a bird, placing all the blame squarely on Chet's shoulders. But there were two sides to every story and this one wouldn't be any different.

Dax and Gage hadn't come out of the conference room yet. They were talking to the federal agents, and Noelle was in a holding cell. Gil was in another holding cell after demanding to see his potion connection, and yes, that is what he called her. I had sent Aunt Mimi a text to see if I could swing by tomorrow to be checked over and she insisted I come tonight at whatever time I left the station. She wanted me to feel wonderful for brunch. So much had happened over the last few days I had forgotten about the party.

Chet was escorted into the police station and I was surprised he wasn't handcuffed. Sharon or Mac must have thought it would be easier to bring him in for questioning if they didn't make it seem dire. He didn't look right or left but kept his head down as he shuffled down the hall between them and into one of the small interrogation rooms. Sharon caught my eye before she closed the door and nodded in the direction of the adjacent room. I went inside and was pleased to see a one-way mirror so I could observe what was happening.

I fidgeted in my seat, my backside getting

sore from the wooden chair. Finally, Gage and Dax entered the observation room, their faces grim. Gage adjusted the speaker volume so we could clearly hear the conversation.

Sharon had a stern look on her face. She had taken on the bad cop role for this interrogation and Mac wore his sympathy face. She said, "Chet, we understand that you were dating Noelle Webber despite the fact that Archie Dane thought he was."

He glared at her. "I can't help it that the man was a fool for her."

"Sounds to me like you both were," she said.

He hung his head. "I shouldn't have done it, but what can I say, I fell in love with her at first sight. Always giving me that megawatt smile and her ever-changing eyes. She hooked me good."

"I understand how a woman can turn your head and make you do crazy things in the name of love?" Mac said. I understood what he was doing, playing the guy connection. "And when did you meet Noelle?"

"In July at the pub in Robin's Pointe, the one Archie was going to all the time hoping to run into her."

"The Magical Moonshine Pub?" he probed.

"Yeah. She came strolling in, this brunette with long hair, eyes a shade of green I had never seen before, and that smile. For the first time, I knew what it meant to be weak in the knees. She toyed with Archie's affection, but I could see she was really into me."

"Then what happened? How did she convince you to start skimming contents from packages?" Peabody's voice was harsh in comparison to Mac's.

"Like all things, it started off as a game, or a dare if you'd like. Could I get away with it? The first item was a pen. Nothing fancy, just one of those pens the electric company sends out every fall. Each time I didn't get caught, she'd up the challenge and she had started seeing Archie too by then. That was when she really tossed me for a loop, said I couldn't get any packages from his mailbag, remove stuff, and put it back in, all without him noticing. But that didn't end well. After I took the pocket watch from Gil Akers and the jewelry from Bee Bee's Boutique, I knew, I was way in over my head but I didn't know how to get out. I came up with the bright idea of dropping Archie's mailbag at the rink, figuring it would get found and someone would investigate." He looked from Sharon to Mac. His palms down on the table and his voice forceful, he said, "But you gotta believe me, I never in a million years thought he'd die."

Peabody's lips formed a thin, hard line. Her voice was clipped as she said, "What happened to the items you took?"

"I gave them to Noelle as proof that I met her challenge." He looked at Mac. "I know, stupid guy doing whatever some girl wants for love."

Peabody said, "Well, this stunt is going to

cost you time behind bars and you've ruined your career and many friendships."

Mac straightened up, his attitude becoming less friendly. "You do know she's blaming you for everything. She's saying after she confided in you about her past, you cooked up the scheme. Do you have anything that can support your side of the story?"

For the first time, Chet perked up. "Yeah, how about the handwritten list from her of whose mail needed to be targeted and what should be in the contents? Before I met Noelle, I would never have done anything like this. Ya gotta believe me."

Mac pushed back from the table and looked at the one-way mirror. It was as if he knew exactly where Gage was standing and then back at Chet. "Why don't you tell me where I can find this note? And before I leave, is there anything else you need to tell us?"

Chet dropped his chin to his chest, the tone of his voice sounded like a broken man. "No, and I might have done some stupid things, but I'd never lie to you, Mac."

I remained in my chair, processing all that we had learned. My brain on information overload. Gage sat down as Sharon had taken Chet from the interrogation room after informing him he was going to be officially booked.

"What are you thinking?"

I clasped my hands in my lap and tilted my head against his shoulder as a wave of sadness washed over me. "How all of this was a waste. It all started with a woman looking for thrills while in witness protection. Noelle single-handedly destroyed three lives plus what is left of her own? Convincing Chet to help her steal, Archie for just being a good guy and wanting to do the right thing, and Gil for being a victim turned vigilante." I took his hand and the warmth from his seeped into me. "I still don't understand why didn't Gil call 9-1-1 instead of leaving Archie bleeding on the ice. He had to have realized the skate caused a serious injury."

He kissed the top of my head. "I can't answer that. The only good news, two crimes were solved today and once again your puzzle-solving skills were crucial to the outcome. If you hadn't been adamant about Noelle, we probably would have taken her at face value and not dug deeper into her background."

"Aw, shucks, Detective. It was just me being a good citizen." I tapped my finger to my chin. "What about the notebooks we found at Archie's apartment? Do you think he was tracking stolen packages?"

Gage smiled. "For once, what we thought was a clue was just a man working on his stamp collection. Oh, and I spoke with Ellen about the argument with Archie the night of the Glow and Glide. She was upset he had encouraged Wyatt to take up stamp collecting. She thinks it's an expensive hobby her son can't afford."

I laughed softly. "Huh. Now that I would

never have guessed, a mailman interested in stamps."

My cell phone pinged with Aunt Mimi's special ringtone. "I need to answer this."

Sitting up straight and before she could demand where I was, I said, "Hi, Auntie. Stop worrying. I'm fine, and we're leaving now. I'll be at your house in under ten minutes." I smiled at Gage and he pointed to his chest. "And Gage said he's coming too."

"Stay for dinner?"

"Thanks, but I am exhausted and want to go home and snuggle with Milo and my handsome fiancé on the sofa with a large pizza."

"Then I'll come to you. The story was busy this afternoon. Nate will be happy to do a pizza run. Besides, I'm hoping we can talk about the party. I mean, the brunch menu for Sunday."

I winked at Gage. "Sure, the more the merrier."

With a promise to bring plenty of pizza, salad, and something for dessert, she hung up.

I gave Gage a small smile. "We're having company for dinner."

"To echo someone I adore, the more the merrier."

Sunday arrived and I had a quiche ready to go to my aunt's place. Gage was arriving any minute. I smoothed down the front of my deep-green velvet dress. It had been an early Christmas present from my mom and I thought it was perfect for today, cozy and comfortable while still being holiday-ish. "Milo, are you ready to go to Aunt Mimi's and Nate's?"

He slunk into the kitchen and stopped in the doorway. "My dear witch, you look lovely for the party."

"Lovely, that is an interesting choice of words."

He wrapped himself in between and around my legs. "All other complements are best left to Detective Cutie. I wouldn't want to steal his magical moment."

I lifted Milo and held him close, kissing the top of his little gray head. "I love you too, Milo. Are you looking forward to brunch today?"

"Now that I learned from Phoenix Mimi has special smoked salmon just for the familiars, yes."

I laughed and gave him a squeeze. "Always thinking of your tummy."

A soft tap on the door drew my attention before it opened. "Gage." He was dressed in well-fitting black jeans, a creamy-beige fisherman knit sweater, and his favorite black cherry cowboy boots. His hazel eyes met mine. My breath caught in my chest.

Milo said for my ears alone, "Take a breath, my dear witch."

"You look very handsome." I crossed the room and kissed his lips. I truly was a lucky woman in so many ways but having Gage Erikson by my side and knowing I would for the rest of my life was the ultimate.

"You're gorgeous." He kissed me again,

causing my heart to flutter like hummingbird wings. "Ready to go?"

I nodded. He picked up my coat and held it for me as I slipped my arms in. We strolled hand in hand down the walkway while I carried Milo and he had the quiche pan. Opening the door to his vintage truck, he helped me inside and kissed me tenderly before he closed the door.

On the short drive to my aunt's place, we held hands. He looked my way. "I was thinking about what happened with Gil. Is it possible to add a charm to your house that if someone comes knocking and wants to do you harm, you'd get some kind of warning?"

Milo tipped his head back from his spot on the seat next to me. "Before you say a word I'll stop you and say, read the book."

I laughed. "How did you know I was going to ask you that question?"

"Because that's what a good familiar is all about, anticipating everything that concerns his witch."

Gage smiled as I laughed. "Did he say something good?"

"He reminded me to read my book, *Practical Beginnings*, which I will do tomorrow. Today we eat, drink, and enjoy time with friends and family."

We pulled up to Aunt Mimi's and the cars that were parked indicated we were the last to arrive. Pushing open my door, I glanced at my watch. "I thought we were right on time but it appears we're late."

Gage took my hand and we stepped on the porch. The bright-red door opened and Aunt Mimi stood in the doorway, her smile as wide as the ocean. "Come in."

The moment our feet crossed the threshold, a loud chorus of "Surprise!" rang out. It was then Gage squeezed my hand and pointed to a banner that hung over the archway. *Happy Engagement!*

Milo jumped down from my arms. "And for the record, I can keep a secret as long as it's for your benefit." He slipped around the corner. I was sure he was in search of his friend and my aunt's familiar, Phoenix, and their special treat.

Aunt Mimi eased me out of my coat. "Come in. It's time we celebrate the happy couple."

Before she could propel us into the throng of well-wishers, I took a step into Gage's arms. "This is just the beginning of a life full of surprises."

A twinkle lit his eyes. "I can't wait, my favorite witch."

If you loved Holidays & Homicide help other readers find this book: **Please leave a review now!**

Are you ready to read more from the Lily and the gang in Pembroke?

**Keep reading for a sneak peek at
Leprechauns & Larceny
A Book Store Cozy Mystery Series
Order Now
Or**

Shop at Lucinda Race

Not ready to stop reading yet? If you sign up for my newsletter at www.lucindarace.com/ newsletter you will receive an excerpt for Cookies & Capers, the introduction of when Lily met Milo right away as my thank-you gift for choosing to get my newsletter.

Leprechauns & Larceny

Chapter 1

Lily

I double-checked the time. It was just noon. I added the notebook to my tote bag. It had a never-ending list of to-do items for the up-coming wedding of my best friends, Nikki and Steve. As the maid of honor, I had taken on the bulk of the last-minute details while Nikki conjured up ideas for her wedding cake. As one of the best kitchen witches in our small town of Pembroke Cove, Maine, I knew it was going to be the most delicious cake ever, even if the theme was St. Patrick's Day and all things Irish. Not that I had a lot to compare it to since I had shied away from weddings. You know the saying always a bridesmaid, never a bride? Well, I thought I was in that category until last fall my forever crush and I finally made it official. Detective Gage Erikson and I started dating and even more recently, we got engaged.

"Milo," I called out to my gray tabby cat, who also happened to be my familiar. He was nowhere to be found. I wandered down the mystery aisle in my bookstore, hoping I'd find him snoozing in the soft kitty bed I had tucked into the corner for him. But it was empty.

"Milo?" He hadn't mentioned he was going out and I needed to get next door to the Pembroke Cove B & B to start decorating for the wedding. The flowers were going to be delivered tomorrow so things needed to get organized. But not before I knew what had happened to Milo.

I stood in the middle of my bookstore with

my hands on my hips and tilted my head back before saying in a loud and clear voice, "Milo, what kind of witch would I be if I left without talking to you?"

"Can't I get a catnap in without being interrupted?" His deep kitty grumble from behind me caught me off guard. I twirled around, thankful I was wearing jeans and not a long skirt which would have tripped me up and I'd be on the floor with my familiar.

"There you are." I scooped him up and crushed him to my chest. "Where were you hiding?"

He tapped his paw, sans claws, to my cheek. "I'm not telling you since I'll never have a peaceful moment when the store is open if you know where to find me."

He rubbed his head under my chin so I knew he was just being cantankerous and not annoyed with me. We had come a long way in the last nine months or so when I discovered I was a witch after my family's book of magic,

Practical Beginnings, had clonked me on the head.

Kissing the space between his ears, I set him in one of the wingback chairs at the front of the store. "I need to run next door and see how the tables are set up for this weekend. Aunt Mimi was going to come down and watch the shop but had something else to do. Not that I know what's more important than this wedding."

"I assume Nikki is up to her wand in icing?" Milo stretched his body across the chair and got comfortable for his next nap.

I couldn't help but laugh. He knew her so well. "She's trying to come up with the perfect flavor combination that not only is fitting for a wedding but will also enhance the theme."

It was only recently that I had discovered wands and witches were a thing. Much to my delight, I had been to a charming shop in Boston called Wanderlings. It was there I selected my wand and I took it with me everywhere. Even now, it was safely tucked into the bottom of my tote bag. Not that I was very good at using it yet, but I would be someday.

He rolled over onto his back and gave me a look. I knew what was coming next.

"I will scratch your tummy later. I'm already late." Slinging my tote bag over my shoulder, I gave him a quick pat. "I'll be back soon so keep an eye on the shop."

"No worries, my dear witch. You can count on me." He yawned and I chuckled. "Maybe I should invest in security cameras to keep a watchful eye." I crossed to the door and my hand was on the knob.

He opened his eyes and looked up again. "Now that's a great idea, or better yet, find the spell that will give you access to your store whenever you want."

"That's a thing?"

He sighed. "Tonight, try asking the book. You've made great progress over the winter, but you might need to challenge yourself in the coming days."

That stopped me in my tracks. "Are you

clairvoyant? Is there something specific I need to be ready for?" Since I discovered my powers, we've had five murders in our sleepy little town and broke up a fraud scheme that had been brewing right under the police department's nose. My newly acquired skills had come into play along with my love of solving puzzles. Thank heavens Gage discovered working with me only helped him solve the cases quicker than without me. In the process, a new witch and our friend, Dax Peters, had moved to town and joined the police force.

"Do you remember what Nikki mentioned at Halloween?"

Racking my brain, I couldn't bring anything to mind except that I had been focused on the haunted house the town put on as a fundraiser, the murder of Mathias Slone, solving said crime, and my almost demise. "You can't mean the casual mention of other kinds of paranormals coming to town."

"Anything is possible and now you need to

hurry. You said it yourself—there is much to do before the big day."

Instantly, kitty snores filled the room. I had to wonder, how did he fall asleep so fast and what did he know that he wasn't telling me? He hinted at information but never divulged the tidbits, letting me discover things as I got into a bit of trouble.

I opened the door and locked it, then added an extra protection charm around the building and Milo. He had become a part of my heart. Not that he wouldn't harass me about that later if he knew, but there was no way I could imagine life without him.

I hurried up the walk and three men dressed like leprechauns grabbed my attention as I slowed my steps. I couldn't make out what they were saying but their tones were laced with anger. They approached a dark SUV parked on the street. As the driver got in, he said, "I am not spending any more time waiting for John Bailey. We agreed and—" The other two men got in, doors slammed, and tires chirped as they pulled away from the curb.

Pushing all thoughts of them aside, I entered Pembroke Cove Bed & Breakfast and it was like stepping back in time to a home from a hundred-plus years ago. A large fireplace dominated one wall of the spacious lobby. There was a small counter for guests to check in and several tables to enjoy afternoon tea or morning coffee completed the space. Katherine Reese-White, the fourth generation of the Reese family to run the inn, was sitting on a small settee near the crackling fire. She looked up and smiled as I closed the oversized wooden door. She was ageless with her porcelain skin unlined, and her red hair cascaded around her shoulders in a riot of curls. I knew she was older than me by at least ten years, but she didn't look it. What she did look like was an advertisement for an Irish lass.

"Lily, this is a surprise. I didn't expect you until later. In fact, I just got back from running errands and I'm taking a few minutes to relax."

She went to get up and I motioned for her to stay seated. "Katherine, relax. I came over to move a few tables around in the dining room. Nikki is working on her cake and asked me to fill in for her."

She pointed to the chair on the opposite side of her. "Join me for a cup of tea first and a cookie from The Sweet Spot. It's your mother's special energy blend and I couldn't resist stopping to see William this morning while I was out. He has the best selection of sweet treats every day."

At the mention of tea and cookies, I eagerly accepted. A cup was just what I needed to power through the rest of the day. And even though my mother wasn't a witch, she had a gift for blending teas that not only fixed what ailed me, but also tasted amazing.

She handed me a delicate china mug and I placed a small sugar cookie on the saucer before I sipped the hot brew, knowing it would slide through my veins and give me a much needed boost.

As we enjoyed our tea and treat, I could tell the tea was working its magic. "This is just perfect. Thank you, Katherine." Sitting by the cozy fire and drinking tea was a rare treat. "Do you enjoy a cup every afternoon?"

"I try to in the winter with the days so long and dark. But along comes St. Patty's Day and the days are getting longer and my days get busier so there's less time to indulge." She smiled over the rim of her cup. "This weekend will be hectic with the out-of-town guests for Nikki and Steve's wedding and we also have some folks in town for the annual parade."

Thinking of a parade with shamrocks and leprechauns wasn't my idea of fun. "How many people usually come up for the events? I thought Boston or even Portland would be better attended than our little town."

She waved her hand in a dismissive nature. "The group is always looking for buried gold. History states that a pirate ship crashed on the coast and the Irish sea captain stashed his gold somewhere in Pembroke Cove. Now the new rumor is the only time it can be found is for three days—March sixteenth through the eighteenth. This year most of the treasure hunters are staying at the motel out on Highway One, but we have four regulars who always stay here. One man, John Bailey, is so enthralled with all things Irish that he stays dressed in costume for the entire event." She smiled. "It's quite a hoot and, of course, it's good for business."

"That sounds interesting but why dress up?"

Her eyes twinkled. "He says it helps him focus in his search for the leprechaun's treasure. I'm not sure if it does, but it's all in good fun."

I was anxious to get into the dining room and start the setup. "Are the wedding preparations I'm doing today going to put a crimp in serving breakfast?"

"Not at all. I'm going to put a small buffet in the sunroom for tomorrow morning."

"Oh, good. Not that we can change the wedding venue at this late date, but since you have guests who come year after year, I wouldn't want to leave a bad taste in anyone's mouth."

"It's a wedding and who doesn't love love?" She swirled her cup and turned the leaves out onto the saucer. "I missed the chance to have you read my tea leaves at the harvest festival. Any chance you'd like to take a peek now?"

The last thing I wanted to do was a reading since the last time I saw a man's bad fortune and he ended up dying. "I can, but I'm not very good at it."

She arched a brow. "That's not what I heard from a few people around town."

My stomach clenched. Did people know I had tried to warn Dean before he left the festival? I shook off the memory. "Think of what you'd like to know, and then we'll look."

"It's important for me to know if my business will continue to do well."

Katherine handed me her cup, I looked and was pleasantly surprised. At the top left of the cup was a cross. At the bottom right, it resembled a cow, and near the handle was a dagger. All in all, not bad.

She scooted forward on the settee. "What do you see?"

I pointed to what I interpreted as a cross. "Here looks to be a bit of trouble, but I wouldn't be too concerned." I pointed to the next area. "This symbol is a dagger which represents help from your friends and the cow in the lower right is a sign for good things to come."

She beamed. "I knew it. When I woke up this morning, I had a feeling that things were going to start going my way for a change."

I wanted to ask her additional questions since that was an odd statement, but I didn't want to pry, even if my curiosity was poking at me to ask. "Is business looking good for the season?"

Katherine knew I was referring to the tourists arriving around Memorial Day through Labor Day. Typically, it was absolutely crazy in town every Friday to Sunday. Once the calendar turned to July and August, the tourists multiplied exponentially. The weather for those two months was as close to perfect as one could enjoy in Maine.

Her smile stretched from ear to ear. "I'm booked solid. In addition to the usual guests, I've even booked two small weddings about the same size as Nikki's. Once she shared with me her ideas, I asked if she'd mind if I borrowed them to promote the inn. Being the sweet lady that she is, Nikki even offered to be the caterer and in-house wedding cake baker too. I think it made all the difference for my reservations."

"That's amazing." I wouldn't be surprised if Nikki had lent a special kind of magical touch to the wedding packages to help Katherine out. She had struggled with the workload the last couple of years since her husband, Donnie, started running treasure hunting charters. He'd be gone for several days at a time, cruising for treasure up and down the coast. He wasn't around much to help with the B & B. Hopefully, having more guests meant a higher cash flow and the ability to hire more help.

As if reading my thoughts, she said, "When I told Donnie the news, he agreed I could hire additional people to help out since he's gone so much during the season."

"Are you looking for more help? I'm sure we could post an ad on the community bulletin board at town hall or maybe even reach out to the high school."

"Lily, what a good idea. I'll stop in at both places tomorrow. With a bit of Irish luck, I might be able to hire a few people and get them trained before the season gets busy. I knew sharing a cup of tea with you would lift my spirits." She got to her feet, "Now, let's go check out that dining room and start pulling it together for a wedding."

I was feeling energetic and ready to pull out my wand, but I wasn't experienced enough yet to use it to create the perfect scene for a wedding—or much else for that matter. Right now, my spell casting was good with one spell at a time.

"Lead the way, Katherine." I slung my bag

over my arm and touched the edge of my book, *Practical Beginnings*. I figured having it with me was a good idea since I never knew when I might need a new spell.

Order today

A Free Story for You

Have you enjoyed Holidays & Homicide? Not ready to stop reading yet? If you sign up for my newsletter at www.lucindarace.com/newsletter you will received Cookies & Capers which is the start of Lily and Milo's adventure as my thank-you gift for choosing to get my newsletter.

Cookies & Capers

I stood in front of the old wood and glass door as I pocketed the keys to the Cozy Nook

Bookshop. Aunt Mimi had signed her bookstore over to me. She said it felt like giving me her baby. But I loved the shop as much as my aunt did. We had worked together for the last twelve years. After attending the University of Maine, I had a degree in history and education. I had always wanted to be a teacher, but jobs were scarce and after substituting for a few years, I moved back to my hometown of Pembroke, Maine, and Aunt Mimi hired me as soon as I unpacked my suitcase.

Spending time with my aunt, learning the business, had been the best experience. I offered to buy the shop when she wanted to retire, but she wouldn't hear of it. As long as she had free books for life, and her long-term boyfriend Nate, she said it was a fair deal. From my point of view, I had built-in backup for years to come.

Now that I was the bookshop owner, Aunt Mimi was no longer coming in every day which meant her cat, Phoenix, wasn't either and the space felt empty without a kitty lying in the window or skulking about as kitties do. I was off to the Pembroke Animal Palace to see if I could find a match.

It was a short walk in the bright noonday sun. The spring air from the ocean carried a tang of salt, but the breeze was refreshing. I waved to one of my best friends, Gage Erikson, as he drove past in his police-issued sedan. My heart fluttered in my chest.

He was a detective on the force. Not that we had much crime in our small seaside town. But one of these days I was going to get brave and tell him I had been carrying a torch for him since we were in ninth grade. What's the worst thing that could happen? We'd still be best friends, right?

I continued down the brick sidewalk, waving to William North from the Sweet Spot Bakery. He was sweeping the area around the small bistro tables in front of the bakery. William was wearing a large pristine white apron and a wide smile. A deep inhale confirmed my suspicion. He was baking cookies.

My mouth watered. I did a half turn and went back to where he was finishing up. "Good morning, William." I bobbed my head in the shop's direction. "What is that tantalizing smell?"

He held open the brightly polished glass door. "One of your favorites, Lily. Chocolate chip and pecan cookies. Can I interest you in one before you continue on your mission?"

I gave him a side-look. "Mission?"

He chuckled. "Over the years my Lulu had said you had two speeds, strolling and purposeful. Just now it was purposeful so hence you're on a mission."

"I'm going to the shelter, hoping to find a kitty. The shop is lonely now that Phoenix is home every day with Aunt Mimi, and I think a cat napping in the window adds an air of serenity to the place."

"Unless you're allergic."

He had a point, but I was not willing to be deterred. I smiled. "I'm always happy to deliver to a customer." I leaned over the glass bakery case, like a kid pressing her nose against the candy case. "You made sugar cookies too and frosted them?" I sighed. I was going to need to exercise more if he continued to bake all my favorites. He was smiling at me as I looked up. "Are the chocolate pecan ready?"

He wiggled his eyebrows. "I have a tray cooling in the back."

"Then can I have one of those and a sugar cookie, but to go?"

With a flick of his wrist, he snapped open a white bakery bag and called over his shoulder. "Jerilyn, would you please bring out the last batch of cookies?"

I heard a muffled, coming, and smiled. "It's good that Jerilyn stayed on." I said nothing about his beloved wife Lulu. Rumor had it she was ill and not doing well.

He nodded. "It is. She's a hard worker and excellent with the customers."

Jerilyn bustled in from the back room carrying a large stainless-steel tray. It was lined with parchment paper and cookies the size of the palm of my hand. It was going to taste so good with a hot cup of tea later.

William put two in the bag, along with two sugar cookies, and then he handed it to me. I paid for my cookies and thanked him. "Stop by the shop later. You might just get to meet my new fur baby."

"Sounds like a plan." He grinned and crossed his arms over his rounded midsection. "You're more like your aunt than you realize. Ever since she opened that bookshop, she's had a cat, too."

I paused, tucked the bakery bag in my tote, and with my hand on the door, I turned and gave him a wide grin. "And now it's time I carry on the tradition." With a jaunty wave, I called, "Wish me luck."

Cookies & Capers is only available by signing up for my newsletter – sign up for it here at www.lucindarace.com/newsletter

Love to read?

**All ebooks and signed paperback copies can be ordered from my website at:
Shop at Lucinda Race**

Cozy Mystery Books
A Bookstore Cozy Mystery Series
<u>Books & Bribes</u>
It was an ordinary day until the book of Practical Magic conked Lily on the head causing her to see stars. And then she discovered her cat, Milo, could talk.

frost and is a long-distance relationship their only option for their second chance?

The Sandy Bay Series
<u>Sundaes on Sunday</u>
A widowed school teacher and the airline pilot whose little girl is determined to bring her daddy and the lady from the ice cream shop together for a second chance at love.

Last Man Standing/Always a Bridesmaid
<u>Barrett</u>
Has the last man standing finally met his match?

<u>Marie</u> *May 2023*
Career focused city girl discovers small town charm can lead to love.

The Crescent Lake Winery Series
<u>Breathe</u>
Her dream come true may be the end of his...
Crush

Love to read?

The first time they met was fleeting, the second time restarted her heart.

Blush

He's always loved her but he left and now he's back...the question, does she still love him?

Vintage

He's an unexpected distraction, she gets his engine running...

Bouquet

Sweet second chances for a widow and the handsome billionaire...

Holiday Romance

The Sugar Plum Inn

The chef and the restaurant critic are about to come face to face.

Last Chance Beach

Shamrocks are a Girl's Best Friend

Will a bit of Irish luck and a matchmaking uncle give Kelly and Tric a chance to find love?

A Dickens Holiday Romance

Holiday Heart Wishes

Love to read?

Heartfelt wishes and holiday kisses...

<u>Holly Berries and Hockey Pucks</u>
Hockey, holidays, and a slap shot to the heart.

<u>Christmas in July</u>
She's the hometown girl with the hometown advantage. Right?

<u>A Secret Santa Christmas</u>
Christmas just isn't Holly's thing, but will a family secret help her find the true meaning of Christmas?

It's Just Coffee Series 2020
<u>The Matchmaker and The Marine</u>
She vowed never to love again. His career in the Marines crushed his ability to love. Can undeniable chemistry and a leap of faith overcome their past?

The MacLellan Sisters Trilogy
<u>Old and New</u>

Love to read?

An enchanted heirloom wedding dress and a letter change three sisters lives forever as they fulfill their grandmothers last request try on the dress.

<u>Borrowed</u>

He's just a borrowed boyfriend. He might also be her true love.

<u>Blue</u>

Will an enchanted wedding dress work its magic one more time?

The Loudon Series

<u>Lost and Found</u>

Love never ends... A widow who talks to her late husband and her handsome single neighbor who has secretly loved her for years.

<u>The Journey Home</u>

Where do you go to heal your heart? You make the journey home...

<u>The Last First Kiss</u>

When life handed Kate lemons, she baked.

<u>Ready to Soar</u>

Love to read?

Kate will fight for love, won't she?
<u>Love in the Looking Glass</u>
Will Ellie's first love be her last or will she become a ghost like her father?
<u>Magic in the Rain</u>
Dani's plan of hiding in plain sight may not have been the best idea.

Social Media

Follow Me on Social Media

Like my Facebook page
Join Lucinda's Heart Racer's Reader Group on
Facebook
Twitter @lucindarace
Instagram @lucindaraceauthor
BookBub
Goodreads
Pinterest

About the Author

ward-winning and best-selling author Lucinda Race is a lifelong fan of reading. As a young girl, she spent hours reading novels and getting lost in the fun and hope they represent. While her friends dreamed of becoming doctors and engineers, her dreams were to become a writer —a novelist.

As life twisted and turned, she found herself writing nonfiction but longed to turn to her true passion. After developing the storyline for A McKenna Family Romance, it was time to start living her dream. Her fingers practically fly over computer keys as she weaves stories of mystery and romance.

Lucinda lives with her two little dogs, a miniature long hair dachshund and a shih tzu mix rescue, in the rolling hills of western Massachusetts. When she's not at her day job, she's immersed in her fictional worlds. And if she's not writing romance or cozy mystery novels, she's reading everything she can get her hands on.